ANNA DePALO

IMPROPERLY WED

Recycling programs
for this product may
not exist in your area.

ISBN-13: 978-0-373-73136-7

IMPROPERLY WED

Bishop Newbury cleared his throat.

"Well, it appears I'm compelled to resort to words that I've never had to use before." He paused. "Upon what grounds do you object to this marriage?"

Colin Granville, Marquess of Easterbridge, looked into her eyes.

"Upon the grounds that Belinda is married to me."

Belinda's eyes narrowed. She could detect mockery in Colin's expression.

Damn him. *He was enjoying this.*

"I'm afraid you must be mistaken," Belinda stated evenly.

Colin looked too sure of himself. "Mistaken about our visit to a wedding chapel in Las Vegas over two years ago? Regrettably, I must disagree."

There was a collective gasp from the assembled guests.

What could she say that wouldn't add to the damage? *I'm sure my brief and secret marriage to the Marquess of Easterbridge was annulled?*

No one was supposed to know about her impetuous and hasty elopement.

* * *

Dear Reader,

With this book, I finally realized my goal of writing a series about aristocratic grooms—all tied together by a wedding disaster.

Belinda Wentworth previously secretly wed her family's sworn enemy, Colin Granville, Marquess of Easterbridge, in Las Vegas. It isn't until her wedding day to another, however, that she discovers—in front of all the guests, no less—that her marriage to Colin was never annulled. The rest, as they say, is history!

If you enjoy the secondary characters in this book, they have their separate stories, which also begin with the day that Colin crashes his own wife's wedding. Tamara and Sawyer featured in *His Black Sheep Bride*, and Pia and Hawk in *One Night with Prince Charming*. I hope you like reading about them!

I am always thrilled to hear from readers. You can email me through my website, www.annadepalo.com, or simply friend me on Facebook or follow me on Twitter, www.twitter.com/anna_depalo.

Best always,

Anna

Recent books by Anna DePalo

Harlequin Desire

Improperly Wed #2123

Silhouette Desire

Having the Tycoon's Baby #1530
Under the Tycoon's Protection #1643
Tycoon Takes Revenge #1697
Cause for Scandal #1711
Captivated by the Tycoon #1775
An Improper Affair #1803
Millionaire's Wedding Revenge #1819
CEO's Marriage Seduction #1859
The Billionaire in Penthouse B #1909
His Black Sheep Bride #2034
One Night with Prince Charming #2075

All backlist available in ebook

ANNA DePALO

A Harvard graduate and former intellectual property attorney, Anna DePalo lives with her husband, son and daughter in New York City. Her books have consistently hit the Borders bestseller list and Nielsen BookScan's list of top 100 bestselling romances. Her books have won the *RT Book Reviews* Reviewers' Choice Award, the Golden Leaf and the Book Buyer's Best, and have been published in more than twenty countries. Readers are invited to reach her at www.annadepalo.com, friend her on Facebook or follow her on Twitter, www.twitter.com/anna_depalo.

This one is for You, the reader,
the reason I write,
and for my editor, Elizabeth Mazer

<u>One</u>

"If any of you can show just cause why they may not lawfully be married, speak now or else forever hold your peace."

Belinda smiled encouragingly at Bishop Newbury.

The reverend returned her smile and opened his mouth to continue…before fixating on something in the pews over Belinda's shoulder.

Belinda heard it then, too. The footfalls sounded ever closer.

No…it couldn't be.

"I object."

Belinda heard the commanding words fall like an anvil on her heart.

A sick feeling gripped her. She closed her eyes.

She recognized that voice—its tone bland but edged with mockery. She'd heard it a million times in her dreams… her most illicit fantasies—the ones that left her blushing and appalled when she woke. And when she hadn't heard it there, she'd had the misfortune of catching it from a distance at a society event or in a television interview or two.

There was a rustling and murmuring in the congregation. Beside her, Tod had gone still. Bishop Newbury looked quizzical.

Slowly, Belinda turned. Tod took his cue from her lead.

Even though she knew what—no, *who*—to expect, her eyes widened as they met those of the man who should have been a sworn enemy to a Wentworth like her. Colin Granville, the Marquess of Easterbridge, heir to the family that had been locked in a feud with hers for centuries... and the person who knew her most humiliating secret.

When her eyes connected with his, she felt longing and dread at the same time. Even under cover of her veil, she could tell there was challenge and possessiveness in his gaze.

He loomed large, even though he wasn't up at the altar with her. His face was hard and uncompromising, his jaw square. Only even features and an aquiline nose saved him from looking harsh.

His hair was the same inky dark brown that she remembered and a shade or two darker than her own chestnut. Brows winged over eyes as dark as they were fathomless.

Belinda raised her chin and met his challenge head-on.

How did one crash a wedding? Apparently, the ticket was a navy business suit and canary-yellow tie. She supposed she should be glad he'd at least settled on formal attire.

Then again, she'd hardly seen Colin the real-estate mogul in anything other than a power suit that did nothing to disguise his athletic build. Well, except for that one night...

"What is the meaning of this, Easterbridge?" her uncle Hugh demanded as he rose from his seat in the first pew.

Belinda supposed someone should be standing to defend the honor of the Wentworths, and Uncle Hugh—as the head of the family—was the logical choice.

She scanned the settled mass of New York and London high society. Her family seemed aghast, but other guests looked fascinated by the unfolding drama.

Her bridesmaids and groomsmen appeared ill at ease, even her friend, Tamara Kincaid, who was always self-assured.

Off to the side of the church, her other close friend and wedding planner, Pia Lumley, had blanched.

"I say, Easterbridge," Tod spoke up, irritated and alarmed. "You were not invited today."

Colin shifted his gaze from the bride to her intended, and his lips curled. "Invited or not, I would hazard to guess that my position in Belinda's life entitles me to a say in these proceedings, wouldn't you?"

Belinda was acutely aware of the hundreds of pairs of interested eyes witnessing the show unfolding at the altar.

Bishop Newbury frowned, clearly perplexed, and then cleared his throat. "Well, it appears I'm compelled to resort to words that I've never had to use before." He paused. "Upon what grounds do you object to this marriage?"

Colin Granville, Marquess of Easterbridge, looked into her eyes.

"Upon the grounds that Belinda is married to me."

As the words reverberated off the soaring walls of the cathedral-size church, gasps sounded all around. Behind Belinda, the reverend began to cough. Beside her, Tod stiffened.

Belinda's eyes narrowed. She could detect mockery in Colin's expression. It lurked in the area around his eyes and in the slight lift to the end of his mouth.

"I'm afraid you must be mistaken," Belinda stated, hoping against hope that she could prevent this scene from getting worse.

As a matter of precise accuracy, she was correct. They had been married oh-so-briefly, but no longer were.

Still, Colin looked too sure of himself. "Mistaken about our visit to a wedding chapel in Las Vegas over two years ago? Regrettably, I must disagree."

There was a collective gasp from the assembled guests.

Belinda's stomach plummeted. Her face felt suddenly hot.

She stopped herself from replying—for what could she say that wouldn't add to the damage? *I'm sure my brief and secret marriage to the Marquess of Easterbridge was annulled?*

No one was supposed to know about her impetuous and hasty elopement.

Belinda knew she had to move this scene to a place where she could face down her demons—or, rather, one *titled* demon in particular—in a less public way. "Shall we resolve this matter somewhere more private?"

Without waiting for a response, and with as much dignity as she could muster, she gathered up the skirt of her wedding dress in one hand and swept down the altar steps, careful not to make eye contact with anyone among the congregated guests as she held her head high.

The sun shone through the church's large stained-glass windows. She walked intermittently through beams of sunlight slanting through the air.

Outside, Belinda knew, it was a perfect June day. Inside, it was another story.

Her perfect wedding was ruined by the man whom family and tradition dictated she should loathe most in the world. If she hadn't been wise enough before to think he was despicable—on that one night in particular—she certainly did now.

When she drew abreast of the marquess, he turned to follow her across the front of the church and through an open doorway that led into a corridor with several doors. Behind Colin, Belinda heard Tod, her erstwhile groom, follow.

When she stopped in the corridor, she heard a louder rustling and murmuring break out in the church. Now that the principal parties had exited the area of worship, she assumed the congregants felt at greater liberty to voice their whispers. She could only hope that Pia would be able to quiet this affair, though she was realistic enough to believe, too, that the effort would be mostly in vain. In the meantime, she could hear Bishop Newbury state to the wedding guests that there had been an unexpected delay.

She ducked into an unoccupied room nearby. Looking around, she concluded from the sparse furnishings and lack of personal belongings that the room probably served as a staging area for church functions.

Turning around, Belinda watched both the groom and her alleged husband follow her into the room. Colin closed the door on the curious faces still looking at them from the main area of the church.

She threw back her veil and rounded on Easterbridge. "How could you!"

Colin was close, and she was practically vibrating with tension, her heart beating loudly. Until now, Colin was the embodiment of her biggest secret and her greatest transgression. She'd tried to avoid or ignore him, but today running was out of the question.

Outrage was, of course, not only the logical but also the easiest emotion to adopt.

"You had better have a good reason for your actions, Easterbridge," Tod said, his face tight. "What possible explanation can you have for ruining our wedding with these outlandish lies?"

Colin looked unperturbed. "A wedding certificate."

"I don't know what alternate reality you've been living in, Easterbridge," Tod replied, "but no one else is amused by it."

Colin merely looked at her and raised an eyebrow.

"Our marriage was annulled," she blurted. "It never existed!"

Tod looked crestfallen. "So it's true? You and Easterbridge are married?"

"We *were*. Past tense," Belinda responded. "And only for a matter of hours, years ago. It was nothing."

"Hours?" Colin mused. "How many hours are in two years? Seventeen thousand four hundred seventy-two, by my calculation."

Belinda rued Colin's facility with math. She'd been stupidly enamored by it—by *him*—at the gaming tables before their impetuous Las Vegas elopement. And now it had come back to haunt her. But how could it be true that they'd been married for the last two years? She'd signed the papers—it was all meant to be wiped away.

"You were supposed to have obtained an annulment," she accused.

"The annulment was never finalized," Colin responded calmly. "Ergo, we are still married."

Her eyes rounded. She was a person who prided herself on remaining unruffled. After all, she'd faced down the occasional recalcitrant client in her position as an art specialist at renowned auction house Lansing's. But if her brief history with Colin was anything to judge by, the marquess had an unparalleled ability to get under her skin.

"What do you mean by *not finalized?*" she demanded. "I know I signed annulment papers. I distinctly remember doing so." Her brow furrowed with sudden suspicion. "Unless you misrepresented what I was signing?"

"Nothing so dramatic," Colin said with enviable composure. "An annulment is more complicated than simply signing a contract. In our case, the annulment papers were not properly filed with the court for judgment—an important last step."

"And whose fault was that?" she demanded.

Colin looked her in the eye. "The matter was overlooked."

"Of course," she snapped. "And you waited until today to tell me?"

Colin shrugged. "It wasn't an issue till now."

She was flabbergasted by his sangfroid. Was this Colin's way of getting back at her for leaving him in the lurch?

"I don't believe this." Tod threw up his hands, his reaction echoing her feelings.

She had decided to proceed without legal counsel in her annulment with Colin, even though she'd had only a cursory understanding of family law. She hadn't wanted anyone—even a family attorney—to know of her incredible lapse in judgment.

Now she regretted the decision not to hire a lawyer. Clearly she'd committed another error in judgment. Not only had she not made sure her annulment had been properly finalized—because she'd wanted to forget about the whole sorry episode in Las Vegas as soon as possible—but as a result she'd put her trust in Colin to see the annulment through.

Colin's gaze swept over her. "Very nice. Certainly a

departure from the red sequin ensemble that you wore during our ceremony."

"Red is an appropriate color when marrying the devil, wouldn't you agree?" she tossed back.

"You didn't act as if I were the devil at the time," he responded silkily, his voice lowering. "In fact, I recall—"

"I wasn't myself," she bit out.

I was out of my mind. That's right, she thought feverishly. Wasn't insanity a basis for annulment almost everywhere?

"Insane?" Colin queried. "Already trying to create a watertight defense to bigamy?"

"I did not commit bigamy."

"Only through my timely intervention."

The man was infuriating. "Timely? We've been married two years according to your calculation."

Colin inclined his head in acknowledgment. "And counting."

She was incredulous at his audacity. But then she supposed that, as her spouse, Colin felt he took precedence over Tod, an *almost* husband. And he'd be right, damn him. Even physically, Colin was more imposing. He was the same height as Tod but more muscular and formidable.

She rued her continuing awareness of Colin as a man. Still, it was a situation she intended to rectify forthwith to the extent she could.

"How long have you known we were still married?" she demanded.

Colin shrugged. "Does it matter if I arrived in time?"

She smelled a rat from his evasive response. *He'd wanted to create a scene.*

Still, he gave nothing away.

"You'll be hearing from my lawyer," she stated.

"I look forward to it."

"We're getting an annulment."

"Not today, however. Not even the state of Nevada works that fast."

He had a point there. Her wedding day was well and truly ruined.

She stared at him in impotent fury. "There are grounds," she insisted, reassuring herself. "I clearly must have been insane when I married you."

"We agreed on lack of consent due to intoxication, you'll recall," he parried.

"Yes, yours!" she retorted, annoyed by his continued sangfroid.

He inclined his head. "By our mutual agreement, due to a better alternative."

"Fraud should have sufficed," she responded tightly. "You completely misrepresented your character to me that night in Las Vegas, and after today, no one would disagree with me. This latest bit of Granville chicanery is for the history books."

He lifted an eyebrow. "Chicanery?"

"Yes," she insisted. "Delivering the news on my wedding day that you were derelict in filing our annulment papers."

"No need to impugn my ancestors by association," he responded calmly.

"Of course, there is," she contradicted. "Your ancestors are why we're in this current mess. They're the reason why—" she gestured in the direction of the church "—the crowd out there was electrified by the news that a Wentworth had married a Granville. What are we going to do?"

"Stay married?" he suggested mockingly.

"Never!"

Belinda turned to exit just as Uncle Hugh and Bishop Newbury barged in.

As she brushed past her uncle, she heard her relative demand, "I hope you have a good explanation, Easter-bridge, though I can't imagine what it is!"

Apparently, all hell had broken loose in the hallowed sanctum.

Revenge.

A sordid word.

Still, revenge hinted at personal animosity. Instead, Colin mused, the Wentworths and Granvilles had been after each other for generations.

Perhaps *feud* or *vendetta* would be more appropriate.

His relationship with Belinda was intimately intertwined with the Wentworth-Granville feud. The feud was the reason that his and Belinda's passion for each other in Las Vegas had been infused with the thrill of the forbidden. It was also why Belinda had run out on him the next morning.

Ever since, he'd been set on a path to make Belinda acknowledge the visceral connection between the two of them—despite the fact that he was a Granville. His plan for doing so involved complicated maneuvers to vanquish the Wentworths, once and for all, and thus end the Wentworth-Granville feud.

Colin gazed at the panoramic view afforded by the floor-to-ceiling windows of his thirtieth-floor duplex condominium, waiting for the visitor who would inevitably arrive. The Time Warner Center, at one end of Columbus Circle, afforded a wealth of privacy as well as luxury to well-heeled foreigners seeking a pied-à-terre in New York City.

He slid his hands into his pockets and contemplated the

treetops of Central Park in the distance. Because it was a Sunday, he was in shirtsleeves rather than a business suit. It was a beautiful sunny day, much as yesterday had been.

Yesterday, of course, was what had almost been his wife's wedding day.

Belinda had appeared divine in her wedding dress, though her expression hadn't been celestial or angelic when she'd confronted him. Rather, she'd looked as if she was torn between cheerfully throttling him and dying of mortification.

Colin smiled at the image that crossed his mind. She had a passionate nature beneath her prepossessed exterior, and it drew him to her. He wanted to strip away the smooth veneer to the substance of the woman beneath.

If yesterday was any indication, Belinda hadn't changed much in two years. She had just as much passion—around him, anyway. Her erstwhile fiancé didn't seem to bring out the same fire. She'd been cool and collected by Dillingham's side, beautiful but detached. The smooth porcelain-doll facade had been in place—at least until he had interrupted the wedding service.

Her rich dark hair had been swept up and away from a face that was still arrestingly lush. Dark brows arched delicately over hazel eyes, an aquiline nose and lips too full for decency. Her ivory wedding dress had hugged a curvaceous figure. Its short lace sleeves and the lace over the décolleté were the only things that saved it from being immodest.

The moment she'd turned away from the altar and toward him, he'd felt a wave of heat and a tightening of the gut, even with the whisper of her veil between them.

Colin clenched his jaw. Belinda had looked breathtaking, just like on their wedding day. But when she'd married him, she'd been full of excitement and anticipation, eyes

alight and those sinful lips spread in a dazzling smile. None
of that stuffy, stilted Wentworth hauteur, just a stunning
blend of passion and sensuality. The remoteness hadn't
emerged until the following morning. But even now, Colin
was pleased to see he could still get a reaction out of her.

After their confrontation in the church staging area,
Belinda had swept out of the room. Colin wouldn't be
surprised if she'd gotten into a cab and gone directly to
her attorney's office. His mocking suggestion that they
remain married had apparently been the last straw, as far
as his wife was concerned.

The wedding reception had gone on, he'd heard.
Belinda's wedding planner and friend, Pia Lumley, had
seen to it at the Wentworth family's request. Regrettably,
however, none of the three principal characters—the bride,
her husband or the groom—had been present.

Colin stared broodingly at the magnificent view from
his windows.

The enmity between the Wentworths and Granvilles
ran deep. The two families were longstanding neighbors,
landowners and, most importantly, rivals in England's
Berkshire countryside. From skirmishes over property
lines to allegations of political treachery and dastardly
seduction of female relations, the flare-ups between the
families had entered into folklore.

He, of course, as the current titular head of the Granville
family, had written a fitting chapter to the long-running
story by eloping in Las Vegas with Belinda Wentworth.

Over the years, he had found Belinda intriguing. Of
course, he'd been curious about her. When he'd seen his
opportunity to get to know her better, he'd taken it—first
at a friend's cocktail party in Vegas and soon afterward,
in a casino.

By the end of the night at the Bellagio casino, he'd

known he wanted Belinda like he'd wanted no woman before her. There had been something about her, and it went beyond the both of them being former competitive swimmers and current opera fans.

She was a dark and striking beauty, more than a match for him in wits. Of course, that same wit was what had made her floor him, as no woman had, at the end of the evening with the announcement that she couldn't sleep with him without a marriage certificate.

Of course, he hadn't been able to resist the challenge. Perhaps his winnings at the gaming tables had made him believe he could win no matter what the odds. He'd been willing to take the gamble for a night in bed with Belinda.

And she *hadn't* disappointed.

He felt a tightening in his gut even now at the memory, more than two years on.

And then yesterday, he'd used the element of surprise to his advantage by crashing Belinda's wedding. He'd only recently discovered that she was to be wed. He'd also guessed that nothing short of a public spectacle would have caused Belinda's wedding plans to fall apart. If he'd given her advance warning, she might have attempted to persuade him to finalize an annulment with no one being the wiser.

Tod Dillingham, who was concerned with status and appearances, would not know how to forgive a public transgression like yesterday. At least, Colin was banking on it.

At the chime of the apartment door, he turned away from the view. *Just in time.*

"Colin," his mother announced as she sailed in, "an incredible rumor has reached me. You must deny it immediately."

Colin stepped aside to let her in. "If it is incredible, why are you here seeking a denial?"

His mother's flair for drama never ceased to amaze him. Fortunately, these days he was usually at a safe remove, since she considered her London flat to be home base. On the other hand, it was his bad luck that a trip of hers to New York in order to visit friends and attend a party or two happened to coincide with Belinda's wedding date. He wondered idly if his younger sister, Sophie, was enjoying a London temporarily free of their mother's presence.

His mother tossed a glance back at him, a sour expression on her face. "Now is no time for you to be jesting."

"Was I?" he mused as he shut the door.

"Tosh! The family name is being besmirched." His mother put down her Chanel bag and settled herself in a chair in the living room, after giving her coat to the housekeeper who magically materialized for a moment. "I demand answers."

"Of course," Colin responded, remaining standing but folding his arms. He acknowledged the housekeeper with a grateful nod.

His mother looked incongruous in the contemporary setting. He was much more used to her in a traditional English sitting room, surrounded by chintz prints and stripes, with old and faded family photos adorning the console table and piano. Certainly she was used to a complete staff of servants.

He and his mother both waited, until his mother raised her eyebrows.

Colin cleared his throat. "What is the rumor precisely?"

"As if you didn't know!"

When he continued to remain silent, his mother sighed with resignation.

"I've heard the most horrible gossip that you disrupted the nuptials of the Wentworth chit. What's more, you apparently announced you were married to her." His mother held up her hand. "Naturally, I cut off the horrible harridan who was repeating the vicious rumor. I informed her that you would never have put in an appearance at a Wentworth wedding. Ergo, you could not have stated that—"

"Who was this teller of tall tales?"

His mother stopped, frowned and then waved a hand dismissively. "A reader of Mrs. Jane Hollings, who writes a column for some paper."

The New York Intelligencer."

His mother looked at him in distracted surprise. "Yes, I believe that's it. She works for the Earl of Melton. Whatever could Melton be thinking to own that rag of a paper?"

"I believe that tabloid turns a healthy profit, particularly online."

His mother sniffed. "It was the downfall of the aristocracy when even an earl went into trade."

"No, World War I was the downfall of the aristocracy," Colin contradicted sardonically.

"You can't possibly have turned up uninvited to the Wentworth nuptials," his mother repeated.

"Of course not."

His mother relaxed.

"When Belinda Wentworth's nuptials actually took place two years ago, I was very much invited—as her groom."

His mother stiffened.

"My station as a marquess, attributable to centuries of proper inbreeding," he continued wryly, "forced me to prevent a crime from being committed when it was within

my means to do so once word reached me of Belinda's
intention to marry again."

His mother sucked in a sharp breath. "Are you saying
that I have been succeeded as the Marchioness of
Easterbridge by a Wentworth?"

"It is precisely what I'm saying."

His mother looked as if she were experiencing vertigo.
The news seemed to hit her with the force of a stock-
market crash. Naturally, Colin had been counting on it;
otherwise she would have been distinctly not amused by
his insouciance.

"I don't suppose she changed her name to Granville in
that chapel in Las Vegas?"

Colin shook his head.

His mother shuddered. "Belinda Wentworth, Marchioness
of Easterbridge? The mind revolts at the thought."

"Don't worry," he offered, "I don't believe Belinda has
used the title or has any intention of doing so."

If Belinda did use the title, his mother would be forced to
style herself as the *Dowager* Marchioness of Easterbridge
in order to avoid confusion. It would be viewed as adding
insult to injury, Colin was sure.

His mother looked exasperated. "What on earth
possessed you to marry a Wentworth in the first place?"

Colin shrugged. "I imagine you could find the answer
among the multitude of reasons that other people get
married." He was unwilling to divulge too much of his
private life to his mother. Like hell was he going to talk
about *passion*. "Why did you and Father marry?"

His mother pressed her lips together.

He'd known his question would end her query. His
parents had married at least partly because they were social
equals breathing the same rarefied air. As far as he could
tell, it hadn't been a bad marriage until his father's death

five years ago from a stroke, but it had been a proper and suitable one.

"Surely you can't mean to stay married."

"Never fear. I wouldn't be surprised if Belinda was consulting her lawyer as we speak."

Colin wondered what his mother would say if she knew that Belinda wanted out of their marriage but he didn't.

At least, not yet—not until his goal was reached.

In fact, he thought, he needed to call his lawyer and find out how the negotiations for his purchase of the property in question were going.

When the deal went through, Belinda would have no choice but to engage him—face matters without running or dodging.

Two

She'd made all the right moves in life...until a night in Las Vegas with Colin Granville.

Belinda tossed a sweater into the suitcase on her bed with more force than necessary.

She'd read history of art at Oxford and then worked at a series of auction houses before landing her current gig as a specialist in impressionist and modern art for posh auction house Lansing's.

She was usually punctual, quietly ambitious and tastefully dressed. She considered herself to be responsible and levelheaded.

In the process, she'd made her family happy. She'd been the dutiful child—if not always doing what they dictated, then at least not rebelling.

She was never the subject of gossip...until this past weekend. One glaring misstep was now the subject of breathless coverage in Mrs. Hollings' Pink Pages column in *The New York Intelligencer*:

It was to be the society wedding of the year.

Except—oh, my!

In case word hasn't reached your tender ears yet, dear reader, this town is abuzz with the news that the Wentworth-Dillingham wedding was crashed by none other than the Marquess of Easterbridge, who proceeded to make the astonishing claim that his short-lived marriage to the lovely Ms. Wentworth two years ago in Las Vegas—of all places!—had never been legally annulled.

Belinda winced as the words from Mrs. Hollings' column reverberated through her mind.

Mrs. Hollings had simply fired the first salvo. *Damn the social-networking sites.* The fiasco at St. Bart's Church had gone viral in the past three days.

She didn't even want to think about her family's continued reaction. She'd avoided calls from her mother and Uncle Hugh in the past few days. She knew she'd have to deal with them eventually, but she wasn't prepared to yet.

Instead, yesterday she'd commiserated over the phone with her closest girlfriends, Tamara and Pia. They'd both been full of sympathy for Belinda's situation, and they'd admitted that the would-be wedding had brought them troubles of their own. Tamara had confessed that she avoided one of the groomsmen at the wedding, Sawyer Langsford, Earl of Melton, because their families had long cherished the idea that the two would wed. Meanwhile, Pia had admitted that she'd discovered one of the wedding guests was her former lover, James "Hawk" Carsdale, Duke of Hawkshire, who had left her without so much as a goodbye after one night three years ago, when he'd presented himself as merely Mr. James Fielding.

In short, the aborted wedding had been a disastrous day for her and her two girlfriends.

Fortunately, Belinda thought, she had a ticket out of town. Tomorrow morning, she would be leaving her tidy little Upper West Side one bedroom for a business trip to England. Even before the wedding that wasn't, she and Tod had decided to postpone a honeymoon for a later date—one that was more convenient for their mutual work schedules. And now she was glad she already had a business trip planned. She couldn't outrun her problems, but some space and distance from the scene of the crime—namely, New York—would help clear her mind so she could come up with a plan.

Ironically, while her wedding date to Tod was supposed to seal her image as the perfect and dutiful society bride, it had done the exact opposite, thanks to Colin's appearance. Her wedding was to have been her apogee, but instead it had been her downfall.

Still, an annulment or divorce should be easy enough to obtain. People got them every day, didn't they? She herself had thought she'd received one.

She paused in the process of packing, sweater in hand, and gazed sightlessly at the clutter on top of her dresser.

She recalled how she'd stared at the annulment papers when they'd arrived for her signature and then pushed aside the quick stab of pain that they had engendered. They were simply a reminder of the blemish on the resume of her life, she'd told herself. But no one needed to know about her appalling mistake.

Belinda dropped the sweater into her suitcase and swallowed against the sudden panicky feeling in the pit of her stomach. She cupped her forehead, as if she could will her proverbial headache away.

But she knew there was no hope of making a six-foot-plus wealthy marquess disappear from her life with a *poof!*

Even before that fateful night in Vegas, she'd run into Colin at social functions occasionally over the years and had found him, well, compelling. But she was too aware of the history between their two families to ever talk directly to him. On top of it all, he was too masculine, too sternly good-looking, too everything. She, who prided herself on her propriety and self-control, couldn't risk spending time with someone who made her feel so…unsettled.

But then she'd been sent on assignment to Las Vegas to appraise the private art collection of a multimillionaire real-estate developer. When she'd run into Colin at the developer's cocktail party, she'd felt compelled for business' sake to socialize with him. She hadn't planned on discovering, much to her chagrin, how charming he was and how much she was attracted to him.

He was like a breath of home in a new place—pleasantly familiar—and yet he stirred a response in her like no one ever had. In the process of idle cocktail party chitchat and banter, she discovered they'd both been standout swimmers in school, they were both partial to operatic performances at New York's Lincoln Center and London's Royal Opera House and they were both active in the same charities to help the unemployed—though Colin sat on the board, while she was more of a foot soldier volunteering her time.

Belinda had thought their similarities were almost disconcerting.

Toward the end of her stay in Vegas, she'd run into Colin again in the lobby of the Bellagio. She'd been momentarily uncertain what to do, but he'd made the decision for her. The ice had already been broken at the recent cocktail party, and what's more, it turned out they were both staying at the Bellagio.

Frankly, she'd been in a partying mood—or at least one for a celebratory drink or two. She'd landed a deal with Colin's real-estate developer friend for a big auction sale of artwork at Lansing's. She knew she had Colin partially to thank. His smooth mediation of her conversations with the developer at the party had certainly been helpful.

Buoyed by a surge in magnanimity, she'd agreed to have a drink with Colin. Their drinks had naturally progressed to dinner and then time at the gaming tables, where she'd been impressed by Colin's winnings.

At the end of the evening, it had seemed like the most natural thing in the world to continue up in the elevator with him to his luxury suite.

She'd teasingly suggested that she couldn't sleep with him unless they were married. She'd gambled on her pronouncement being the end of the matter. After all, she'd recently broken up with a boyfriend of more than a year with nothing to show for it.

Colin, however, had shocked her by upping the ante and daring her to go to the Las Vegas Marriage License Bureau with him. They'd turned around and headed back downstairs.

She'd been by turns amused and horrified by their escapade, especially when they'd started hunting for a chapel. She'd never been in an iconic Las Vegas wedding chapel. One had been too easy to find that night.

Later, of course, she'd blame her uncharacteristic actions on having had a drink or two and on the crazy Vegas environment. She'd point the finger at just having turned thirty and losing another boyfriend. She'd place fault on the increasing pressure from her family to marry well and soon, and on the fact that most of her wellborn classmates from Marlborough College were already engaged or married. She'd even blame her surge of goodwill toward Colin, who'd helped her land business at the cocktail party. Basically, she'd found everyone and everything at fault—most of all herself.

In the morning, her cell phone had rung, and she'd blearily identified the call as being from her mother. It had been as if someone had doused her with icy water while she'd still been half-asleep. She'd come back to reality with a shock, and had been truly horrified by what she'd done the night before. She'd insisted on a quick and quiet annulment without anyone being the wiser.

At first, Colin had been amused by her alarm. But soon, when it had become clear that her distress wasn't temporary, he'd become closed and aloof, thinly masking his anger.

Belinda dropped her hand from her forehead, and in the next moment, she was startled by the ring of her cell phone.

She sighed. She supposed it was a good thing to be jostled out of unhappy memories.

Locating the phone on top of her dresser, she confirmed what the ring tone was telling her—it was Pia calling.

She put a Bluetooth device in her ear for hands-free listening so she could continue packing while she talked.

"Aren't you supposed to be in Atlanta for a wedding?" Belinda asked without preamble once she had her earpiece in place.

"I am," Pia responded, "but I have until the end of the week before the pace picks up for Saturday's main event."

She and Pia and their mutual friend, Tamara, had gotten to know each other through charitable work for the Junior League. All three of them had settled in New York in their twenties, soon after university. Though they'd chosen to live in different Manhattan neighborhoods, and were busy pursuing different careers—Tamara's being in jewelry design while wedding planning had always been Pia's dream—they had become fast friends.

Though Tamara was the daughter of a British viscount, Belinda had not met her as part of the aristocratic set in England because Tamara had grown up mostly in the United States, after her American-born mother had divorced her titled husband. Too bad—her free-thinking bohemian friend would have been a breath of fresh air in Belinda's stilted, structured adolescence. Tamara had never met a trend that she didn't want to buck—a trait that Belinda couldn't help but admire. Pia was more like herself, though her friend came from a middle-class background in rural Pennsylvania.

"Don't worry," Belinda joked, guessing the reason for Pia's call, "I'm still alive and kicking. I intend to be granted my freedom from the marquess if it's the last thing that I do."

"Oh, B-Belinda, I-I-I wish there was something I could do," Pia said, her stutter making a rare appearance.

"Colin and I made this mess, and we'll have to be the ones to clean it up."

Belinda regretted the repercussions for Pia's wedding-planning business from the nuptial disaster on Saturday. She'd thought only of helping her friend's career when she'd asked Pia to be her wedding planner instead of her bridesmaid—despite knowing Pia was a dyed-in-the-wool romantic. Unfortunately, none of her plans for Saturday had worked out well.

Damn, Colin.

Since she'd had a three-way phone conversation with Pia and Tamara only yesterday, and Pia had just arrived in Atlanta for business today, Belinda sensed there might be more reason for her friend's call than an opportunity to chat.

Because she was not one to skirt an issue, unless it involved her *husband*—not to be confused with her *groom*—she went straight to the point. "I know you wouldn't be calling without a reason."

"W-well," Pia said delicately, "I wish this conversation could take place at a later time, but there is the issue of what announcement to send, if any, with regard to Saturday's, er, interrupted nuptials. And then, of course, the wedding gifts—"

"Send them all back," Belinda cut in.

She was an optimist but also a realist. She didn't know for sure how long it would take to bring the marquess to heel at least long enough to grant her an annulment or divorce.

"Okay." Pia sounded relieved and uncertain at the same time. "Are you sure, because—"

"I'm sure," Belinda interrupted. "And as far as a statement, I don't think one is necessary. A wedding announcement would no longer be appropriate obviously, and anything else would be unnecessary. Thanks in part to Mrs. Hollings, I believe everyone is in the know about Saturday's events."

"What about you and Tod?" Pia asked. "Will you be able to, ah, patch things up?"

Belinda thought back to the events of Saturday.

Outside the church, Tod had caught up with her, apparently having exited the confrontation with Colin soon after she had. They'd had a short and uncomfortable conversation. While he had tried to maintain a stiff upper lip, Tod had still seemed flabbergasted, annoyed and embarrassed.

She'd handed his engagement ring back to him. It

had seemed like the only decent thing to do. She'd just discovered she was still married to another man, after all.

Then she had ducked into the white Rolls Royce at the curb, relieved to have attained privacy at last. She had been quivering with emotion ever since Colin's voice had rung out at the church.

Belinda sighed. "Tod is perplexed and angry, and under the circumstances, I can hardly blame him."

She winced when she thought about her glaring omission—not telling him about her elopement. Her only excuse was that she could hardly bear to think about it herself. It was too painful.

She hadn't been able to live down her uncharacteristic behavior, and then it had come barging in in the form of a tall, imposing aristocrat who aroused passionate reactions in her.

Pia cleared her throat. "So matters between you and Tod are...?"

"On hold. Indefinitely," Belinda confirmed. "He's waiting for me to resolve this situation, and then we'll decide where we'll go from there."

Pia said nothing for a moment. "So you don't want to issue any public statement...for clarification?"

"Are you volunteering to be my publicist?" Belinda joked.

"It wouldn't be the first time I issued a public statement or a press release for a bride," Pia responded. "Media relations is part of the job for society wedding planners these days."

Belinda sighed. "What could I say, besides confirming that I am in fact still married to Easterbridge?"

"I see your point," Pia conceded, "and I don't disagree. But I thought I'd give you the opportunity to respond to Mrs. Hollings if you want to."

"No, thanks."

The last thing Belinda wanted was for this scandal to play out in the media. After all, a public statement by her might just invite Easterbridge to issue his own *clarifications.*

She would try to deal with Colin privately and discreetly—even if she had to go beard the lion in his den. She wanted to avoid further scandal, if possible. She knew it was a slippery slope from retaining lawyers to sending threatening letters and ultimately going through an ugly and public divorce.

"What the devil has gotten into you, Belinda?" Uncle Hugh said, coming around his desk as Belinda stepped into the library of his town house in London's Mayfair neighborhood.

The mark of disapproval was stamped all over her uncle's face.

She was being called to account. She, Belinda Wentworth, had done what none of her ancestors had—betrayed her heritage by marrying a Granville.

Belinda knew when she'd gone to London on business that she'd be compelled to pay a visit at the Mayfair town house. She had been able to escape in-depth conversations—and explanations—with her relatives directly after the wedding by departing the church forthwith and having Pia run interference for her at the show-must-go-on reception afterward. Her family had also been preoccupied with trying to save face with the assembled guests—to the extent such a thing was possible.

She glanced above the mantel at the Gainsborough painting of Sir Jonas Wentworth. The poor man was probably turning in his grave.

The London house had been in the Wentworth clan

for generations. Like many other highborn families, the Wentworths had fought tooth and nail to hang on to a fashionable Mayfair address that carried a certain cache, if no longer necessarily signifying generations of quality breeding due to the growing number of new money.

Though the Wentworths were not titled, they descended from a younger branch of the Dukes of Pelham and had intermarried with many other aristocratic families over the years—save, of course, for the despised Granvilles. Thus, they considered themselves as blue-blooded as anybody.

"This is quite a tangle that you've created," her uncle went on as a servant rolled in a cart bearing the preparations for afternoon tea.

Belinda worried her bottom lip. "I know."

"It must be resolved forthwith."

"Of course."

As the servant left the room, Uncle Hugh gestured for Belinda to sit down.

"Well, what are you going to do to fix this mess?" he asked as they both sat, she on the sofa and he in a nearby armchair.

By force of habit, Belinda leaned forward to fix tea. It gave her something to do—and the illusion of being in control while not meeting Uncle Hugh's gaze.

"I intend to obtain an annulment or divorce, of course," she said evenly.

Despite her self-assured attitude, there was nothing *of course* about it.

She surveyed the tea tray. A proper English tea was more than loose tea and hot water. There were the customary finger sandwiches, buttery biscuits and warm scones.

Really, she could drown herself in scones right now. Crumbly blueberry ones...rich raisin ones...decadent chocolate-chip ones—

No, not decadent. Definitely not decadent. It came too close to mimicking the behavior that had gotten her into her current fix with Colin.

She was decidedly not into decadent behavior, she told herself firmly.

Nevertheless, an image flashed into her mind of lounging on a king-size bed with Colin Granville, sharing champagne and strawberries high above the flashing lights of Las Vegas.

Her face heated.

"…a youthful indiscretion?"

She fumbled in the process of pouring hot water into a cup.

She jerked her head up. "What?"

Her uncle raised his eyebrows. "I was merely inquiring whether this unfortunate situation came about due to a youthful indiscretion?"

She knew she must look guilty. "Can I claim so even though I was thirty at the time?"

Uncle Hugh regarded her with a thoughtful but forbearing expression. "I'm not so old that I don't remember how much partying and club-hopping can go on in one's twenties or beyond."

"Yes," Belinda said, more than ready to accept the proffered excuse. "That must be it."

Her uncle accepted a teacup and saucer from her.

"And, yet, I'm surprised at you, Belinda," he went on as he took a sip of his tea. "You were never one for rebellion. You were sent to a proper boarding school and then to Oxford. No one expected this scenario."

She should have guessed that she would not be let off the hook so easily.

Belinda stifled a grimace. Marlborough College's most famous graduate these days was the former Kate

Middleton, Duchess of Cambridge, who would mostly likely be queen one day. *She,* by startling contrast, had failed miserably on the matrimonial front. She now had the wreckage of not one but two wedding ceremonies behind her.

She hated to disappoint Uncle Hugh. He had been a father figure to her since her own father's death after a yearlong battle with cancer when she'd been thirteen. As her father's older brother, and the head of the Wentworth family, her uncle had fallen naturally into the paternal role. A longtime widower, Uncle Hugh had been unable to have children with his wife and had remained single and childless since then.

On her part, Belinda had tried to be a good surrogate daughter. She'd grown up on Uncle Hugh's estates— learning to swim and ride a bicycle during her summers there. She'd gotten good grades, she hadn't acted out as a teenager and she'd kept her name out of the gossip columns—until now.

Uncle Hugh sighed and shook his grayed head. "Nearly three centuries of feuding and now this. Do you know your ancestor Emma was seduced by a Granville scoundrel? Fortunately, the family was able to hush up matters and arrange a respectable marriage for the poor girl to the younger son of a baronet." His eyebrows knitted. "On the other hand, our nineteenth-century land dispute with the Granvilles dragged on for years. Fortunately, the courts were finally able to vindicate us on the matter of the proper property line between our estate and the Granvilles'."

Belinda had heard both stories many times before. She opened her mouth to say something—*anything*—about how her situation with Colin was different.

"Ah! I see I've finally run you to ground."

Belinda turned in time to watch her mother sail into

the room. She abruptly clamped her mouth shut to prevent herself from groaning out loud. *Out of the frying pan and into the fire.*

Her mother handed her purse and chiffon scarf to a servant who hastened in from the doorway before turning for a discreet retreat. As usual, she looked impeccably turned out—as if she'd just come from lunch at Annabelle's or one of her other customary jaunts. Her hair was coiffed, her dress was timelessly chic and probably St. John and her jewels were heirlooms.

Belinda thought that the contrast between her and her mother could hardly be more pronounced. She was casually dressed in chain-store chinos and a fluttery short-sleeved blouse that were paired with a couple of Tamara's affordable jewelry pieces.

Even aside from the accoutrements, however, Belinda knew she did not physically resemble her mother. Her mother was a fragile blonde, while she herself was a statuesque brunette. She took after the Wentworth side of the family in that regard.

"Mother," Belinda tried, "we spoke right after the wedding."

Her mother glanced at her and widened her eyes. "Yes, darling, but you gave me only the vaguest and most rudimentary of answers."

Belinda flushed. "I told you what I knew."

Her mother waved a hand airily. "Yes, yes, I know. The marquess' appearance was unexpected, his claims outlandish. Still, it all begs the question as to how precisely you've been married two odd years with no one being the wiser."

"I told you the marquess claims that an annulment was never finalized. I am in the process of confirming that claim and rectifying matters."

She had not hired a divorce lawyer yet, but she had phoned an attorney in Las Vegas, Nevada, and requested that Colin's claim be verified—namely, she and Colin were still married.

Her mother glanced at Uncle Hugh and then back at her. "This scandal is the talk of London and New York. How do you plan to rectify that matter?"

Belinda bit her lip. Obviously, her mother, having met with resistance to her first line of inquiry, had moved on to another.

It was ironic, really, that she was being subjected to questioning by her mother. She had turned a deaf ear to her mother's personal affairs over the years, though they had been the subject of gossip and cocktail-party innuendo. She hadn't wanted to know more about *affaires de coeur*, as her mother was fond of referring to them.

Her mother looked fretful. "How will we ever resolve this with the Dillinghams? It's disastrous."

"Now, now, Clarissa," her uncle said, leaning forward to set down his teacup. "Histrionics will not do a bit of good here."

Belinda silently seconded the sentiment and then heaved an inward sigh. She and her mother had never had an easy relationship. They were too different in personality and character. As an adult, she'd been pained when her mother's behavior had been shallow, selfish or self-centered, and often all three.

As if on cue, her mother slid onto a nearby chair, managing somehow to be graceful about it while still giving the impression that her legs would no longer support her during this ordeal. "Belinda, Belinda, how could you be so reckless, so irresponsible?"

Belinda felt rising annoyance even as she acknowledged

she'd been asking herself the same question again and again. She *had* acted uncharacteristically.

"You were expected to marry well," her mother went on. "The family was counting on it. Why, most of your classmates have already secured advantageous matches."

Belinda wanted to respond that she *had* married well. Most people would say that a rich and titled husband qualified as good enough. And yet, Colin was a detested Granville and thus one who was not to be trusted under any circumstances.

"We spent a long time cultivating the Dillinghams," her mother continued. "They were prepared to renovate Downlands so you and Tod might entertain there in style once you were married."

Belinda didn't need to be reminded of the plan, contingent on her marriage to Tod, to update the Wentworths' main ancestral estate in Berkshire. She knew the family finances were, if not precarious, less than robust.

Truth be told, neither she nor Tod had been swept away by passion. Instead, their engagement had been based more on practicalities. She and Tod had known each other forever and had always gotten along well enough. She was in the prime of her friends' matrimonial season, if not toward the end of it, at thirty-two. Likewise, she knew Tod was looking for and expected to marry a suitable woman from his highborn social set.

Tod had said he would wait for her to resolve the situation. He had not said how long he would wait, however.

Her mother tilted her head. "I don't suppose you could lay claim to part of Easterbridge's estate for being accidentally married for the past two years?"

Belinda was appalled. "Mother!"

Her mother widened her eyes. "What? There have been plenty of real marriages that have endured for less time."

"I'd have more leverage if Easterbridge were divorcing me!"

Belinda recalled the marquess' jesting offer to remain married. It was clear she'd have to be the one to initiate proceedings to dissolve their marriage.

"You didn't have time to sign a prenuptial agreement at that wedding chapel in Las Vegas, did you?" her mother persisted and then sniffed—ready to answer her own question. "Why, I wouldn't be surprised if Easterbridge carried a standard contract in his back pocket."

"Mother!"

Uncle Hugh shook his head. "A man as sharp as Easterbridge would have seen to it that his property was not vulnerable. On the other hand, we wouldn't want the marquess to make any claim to Wentworth property."

Her mother turned back to her. "It's a good thing that none of the Wentworth estates are in your name."

"Yes," Uncle Hugh acknowledged, "but Belinda is an heiress. She stands to inherit the Wentworth wealth. If she remains Easterbridge's wife, her property may eventually become his to share, particularly if the assets are not kept separate."

"Intolerable," her mother declared.

For her part, Belinda didn't feel like an heiress. In fact, from all of her family's focus on making a good match, she felt more stifled than liberated by the Wentworth wealth. True, she was the beneficiary of a small trust fund, but those resources only made it bearable for her to live in Manhattan's high-rent market on her skimpy art specialist's salary.

She'd been reminded time and again that her task was to carry the Wentworth standard forward for another generation. She was never unaware of her position as an only child. So far, however, she could not have made a bigger mash of things.

"I'll deal with the marquess," Belinda said grimly, stopping herself from her nervous habit of chewing her lip.

Somehow, she had to untangle herself from her marriage.

Three

"Thank you for meeting me today," she said, somewhat incongruously, as she stepped into a conference room in Colin's business offices at the Time Warner Center.

She was hoping to keep matters on a polite and productive footing. Or at least to start that way.

Colin gave a quick nod of his head. "You're welcome."

Belinda watched as Colin's gaze went unerringly to her now ring-free hand.

Her heart beat loudly in her chest.

She'd wanted a meeting place that was private but not too private. She knew Colin owned a spectacular penthouse high above them in the same complex—it was one of the unavoidable pieces of information that she'd come across about him in the news in the past couple of years—but she'd shied away from facing him there. And her own apartment farther uptown was too small.

It would have been hard enough to confront Colin under

any circumstances. He was wealthy, titled and imposing—not to mention savvy and calculating. But he was also her former lover and could lay claim to knowing her intimately. Their night together would always be between them. She'd seen what they could do with a hotel room… What they could do in his apartment didn't bear thinking about. At all. Ever.

Belinda scanned him warily.

He wore a business suit and held himself with the easy and self-assured charm of a sleek panther ready to toy with a kitty. He carried the blood of generations of conquerors in his veins, and it showed.

Belinda felt awareness skate over her skin, a good deal of which was exposed. She was dressed in a V-neck belted dress and strappy sandals, having arranged to have this meeting during her lunch break at Lansing's.

Colin gestured to the sideboard. "Coffee or tea?"

She set down her handbag on the long conference table. "No, thank you."

He perused her too thoroughly. "You are rather even-keeled, in sharp contrast to last week."

"I've chosen to remain the calm in the storm," she replied. "The rumors have run amok, the groom has decamped for the other side of the Atlantic and the wedding gifts are being returned."

"Ah." He sat on a corner of the conference table.

"I hope you're satisfied."

"It's a good start."

She quelled her ire and looked at him straight on. "I am here to make you see reason."

He was ill-mannered enough to chuckle.

"I know you're busy—" *too busy to have obtained an annulment, obviously* "—so I'll go straight to the point. How is it possible that we're still married?"

Colin shrugged. "The annulment was never finalized with the court."

"That's what you said." She smelled a rat—or more precisely, a cunning aristocrat. "I hope you fired your lawyer for the matter."

She took a steadying breath. The lawyer she had recently consulted had confirmed that, as far as state records showed, she and Colin were still married because there was no record of an annulment or even of papers being filed.

One way or the other, she had to deal with matters as they unfortunately stood.

"It's futile to look back," Colin remarked, as if reading her mind. "The issue is what do we do now."

Belinda widened her eyes. "Now? We obtain an annulment or divorce, of course. New York recently did me the enormous favor of introducing no-fault divorce, so I'll no longer have to prove that you committed adultery or abandoned me. I know that much from some simple research."

Colin looked unperturbed. "Ah, for the good old days when marriage meant coverture and only a husband could own property or prove adultery."

She didn't appreciate his humor. "Yes, how unfortunate for you."

He lifted his lips. "There's only one problem."

"Oh? Only one?" She was helpless to stop the sarcasm.

Colin nodded. "Yes. A no-fault divorce can still be contested, starting with the service of divorce papers."

She stared at him dumbly. What was he saying?

She narrowed her eyes. "So you're saying..."

"I'm not granting you an easy divorce, in New York or anywhere else."

"You ruined my wedding, and now you're going to ruin

my divorce?" she asked, unable to keep disbelief from her voice.

"Your wedding was already ruined because we were still married," Colin countered. "Even if I hadn't interrupted the ceremony, your marriage to Dillingham would have been considered void ab initio due to bigamy. It would have been as if the marriage ceremony had never occurred."

Belinda pressed her lips together.

Colin raised an eyebrow. "I know. It's rather inconvenient that your marriage to Dillingham would have been the one to have been declared legally nonexistent."

"You ruined my wedding," she accused. "You chose the precise wrong moment to make your big announcement. Why crash the ceremony?"

"Shouldn't you be thanking me for preventing a crime from being committed?"

She ignored his riposte. "And to top it off, you ruined my marriage by not making sure the annulment was properly finalized."

"Your marriage to whom? The one to Tod that never existed? Or ours? Most people would say that not finalizing an annulment is the way to avoid ruining a marriage."

She wasn't amused by his recalcitrance. She'd come here to get him to agree to a quiet dissolution of their union.

Colin rubbed his chin. "I can't understand how you managed to keep our Las Vegas wedding a secret. Did Dillingham even know?"

Belinda reddened. "Tod is standing by me."

"That means no." Colin let his gaze slide over her hand. "Also, you're not wearing his ring. Just how...*closely* is he standing by? Or does his support amount to waiting in the wings until this whole messy divorce business is taken care of? But just how long is he willing to wait?"

"As long as it takes," she shot back.

They stared at each other, and Belinda forced herself not to blink. The truth was she had no idea how long or how short Tod would wait. The wedding fiasco had been quite a blow.

Colin tilted his head and contemplated her. "You didn't even tell him that you already had one wedding behind you. Were you afraid of what an Old Etonian like Dillingham would think of the quick Vegas elopement in your past?"

"I'm sure he would have been bothered only by the fact that the groom had been you," she retorted.

"Right, competitive," Colin said, nodding even as he twisted her meaning. "But then there's the fact that you lied on your marriage license."

Belinda's flush deepened.

It was true that she had omitted to list the Las Vegas ceremony when applying for a marriage license in New York. Her union with Colin had been a marriage of brief duration that had been contracted in another state and, she believed, had ended in an annulment.

Didn't an annulment usually mean that a marriage had never existed?

Belinda rallied her reserves.

"You know quite a bit about dissolving a marriage even if you haven't accomplished it successfully yourself," she retorted. "Have you talked to a lawyer already?"

"You have. Why shouldn't I?" he returned rather cryptically.

"That's the difference between you and Tod. He hasn't spoken with an attorney." The last thing she needed was for the Dillinghams to resort to legal means to recoup their costs for the wedding fiasco.

Colin twisted his lips. "Pity. Because if he had, his lawyer would have told him just what my lawyer told me.

If I choose to fight your divorce suit, you'll remain my wife for quite a while longer."

"So you plan to fight it?"

"With everything I've got."

"I'll win eventually."

"Maybe, but I'm sure the Wentworths won't appreciate the notoriety."

He was right, Belinda thought with a sick feeling. If this scandal deepened, her family would be horrified. And she felt ill just thinking of the Dillinghams' reaction.

"You're the Marchioness of Easterbridge," Colin said, driving his point home. "You might as well start using the title."

Marchioness of Easterbridge. She was glad her ancestors weren't around to hear this.

"It's a good thing you chose to keep your surname on the Nevada marriage license," Colin continued. "Otherwise, you'd have been erroneously representing yourself as Belinda Wentworth rather than Belinda Granville for more than two years."

"I remember choosing to keep my name," she shot back. "I wasn't so completely off kilter that I don't remember that detail."

Somehow, it had been acceptable to marry Colin but not to take the Granville name.

Belinda Granville. It sounded worse than Marchioness of Easterbridge. Easterbridge was simply Colin's title, whereas Granville had been the surname carried by his devious ancestors.

"Why are you doing this?" she blurted. "I can't understand why we shouldn't have a civilized divorce—or better yet, annulment."

He sauntered toward her. "Can't you? Nothing has been civilized between the Wentworths and the Granvilles for generations. The ending of our…encounter in Las Vegas is further evidence of it."

Her eyes widened. "So it all goes back to that, doesn't it?"

He stopped before her. "I intend to make a conquest of the Wentworths once and for all—" his gaze slid down her body "—beginning and ending with you, my beautiful wife."

Disaster preparedness.

He'd laid the groundwork, Colin thought. He'd spent two-plus years planning for this moment, making sure he'd anticipated every likely contingency.

"Excellent," Colin said into the phone. "Did he ask many questions?"

"No," his deputy responded. "Once he knew you were willing to meet his price, he was pleased."

And now, he was satisfied himself, Colin thought.

"I believe he assumed you were a Russian oligarch looking to make a prime purchase."

"Even better," Colin replied.

If he knew Belinda, in the past few weeks she'd been quietly working to find a way to disengage herself from their union with as little fanfare as possible. But now he held a trump card.

After ending the call, he looked up at his two friends. When his cell phone had buzzed, and he'd seen who was calling, he'd been too impatient for answers to ignore the call despite the presence of company on a Thursday evening.

From their seats in upholstered chairs in the sitting room of Colin's London town house, Sawyer Langsford, Earl of Melton, and James Carsdale, Duke of Hawkshire, exchanged looks. They all happened to be in town at the same time and had met for drinks. Having removed their jackets, they all sat around with loosened ties.

Like his two fellow aristocrats, Colin had had a more peripatetic existence than most, so his accent was cosmopolitan rather than British. Still, despite all being well-traveled—or maybe, because of it—he, Sawyer and Hawk had become friends. Thus it seemed oddly appropriate that the three of them would become romantically entangled at the same time.

Sawyer had unexpectedly gotten engaged to Tamara Kincaid, one of Belinda's bridesmaids. Hawk was intently pursuing Pia Lumley, Belinda's wedding planner, in an effort to smooth out his bumpy history with her.

Both of his friends were enjoying rather more success romantically than Colin at the moment—though unsurprisingly, Belinda's friends had proven challenging to woo, as well. Colin had an advantage in that Belinda was already his wife. Yet the fact that she now refused to communicate with him except through lawyers was a decided obstacle.

But no matter. He and Belinda were still married, and with his business deal today, she'd have to deal with him sooner rather than later.

"What game are you playing, Easterbridge?" Hawk inquired.

"A rather high-stakes one, I'm afraid," Colin said in a faintly bored tone. "I'm sure you want no part of it."

Hawk raised an eyebrow.

Sawyer shrugged. "You've always played your cards close to your chest, Colin."

"Simply doing my best to burnish the Granville surname." And what better way to varnish it than to be responsible for finally vanquishing the family foes, the Wentworths?

Colin hadn't given much thought to his fellow Berkshire landowners over the years. This was the twenty-first century, after all, and civility toward one's neighbors, barring direct provocation, was the norm. Besides, in his rather small aristocratic world, it was considered downmarket to openly not get along.

He'd been willing to let bygones be bygones for most of his thirty-seven years, not interacting with the Wentworths but not engaging in open feuding, either. He'd been disposed to maintain a status quo of wary distance because not much had been at stake.

But then he'd unexpectedly come into contact with Belinda in Las Vegas. He was as susceptible as the next man to a leggy brunette with flashing eyes.

He'd been intrigued by Belinda Wentworth whenever he'd occasionally chanced to cross her path over the years. It hadn't happened often. She was a good half-dozen years younger, so their childhoods in Berkshire had not overlapped much. He'd been sent up to Eton at the age of thirteen to continue his studies, and had only rarely returned home. By the time he'd begun to establish his real-estate empire, Belinda had been off at school herself.

But then, an opportunity had presented itself at a Vegas cocktail party to speak with Belinda and he'd been pleased, not least of all because his curiosity had been stoked.

Nothing had happened that night but banter and conversation, but it had definitely whetted his appetite for more. When he'd encountered Belinda in the hotel lobby of the Bellagio, a couple of days after the cocktail party, he hadn't let the opportunity that he'd been hoping for slip by. He'd invited her to have a drink. Drinks had become dinner, and then they'd wound up in the casino, where he'd been able to exhibit his skill at the gaming tables.

By that time, of course, he'd *really* wanted Belinda.

She'd been a desirable woman who pushed all the right buttons for him. By the end of the night, he'd had a sense of rightness and anticipation.

She'd followed him into the elevator leading to his luxury suite. But then she jokingly suggested that she'd have to marry him first.

The gauntlet had been thrown down.

He'd studied her. She looked relaxed and uninhibited but not as if she'd crossed the line to being intoxicated.

The elevator doors opened, and they stepped out onto the penthouse floor.

He turned to her and took a step closer.

"It doesn't seem right to marry you when I haven't even kissed you," he murmured in a low voice.

Belinda's hazel eyes twinkled. "I'm not putting out anymore without a promise. You know, like the song 'Single Ladies.'"

Her tone was joking, but he detected an underlying note of seriousness.

"Someone hurt you."

She shrugged. "Not badly."

Colin experienced a sudden surge of anger at an unnamed jerk.

Blast, he was far gone.

One kiss.

He cupped Belinda's face and ran his thumb over her mouth. She closed her eyes on a sigh, and he bent his head to sip from her pink lips.

She tasted sweet, so sweet. Their breaths mingled.

He sunk into the kiss, heedless of the fact that they were next to the elevator and the doors could open at any moment.

He'd always been daring. He'd had to take risks to expand his real-estate empire. In his personal life, he'd skydived, bungee jumped and usually done whatever was the thrill in vogue—much to the chagrin of his mother, who hadn't liked seeing the heir or, subsequently, the holder of the marquessate, risking his neck.

"This is Vegas, and you know what that means," he said after the kiss ended.

Belinda had looked at him inquiringly.

"There must be a wedding chapel nearby."

The lark had started that way and just gained momentum.

They'd gone downstairs again, and sure enough, they'd located a wedding chapel without too much trouble.

He'd never met a woman before who was willing to up the ante with him. It was a powerful aphrodisiac.

And then back at the hotel, when they'd finally gone to bed, she'd stunned him with how natural and uninhibited she was.

In the morning, however, he'd been met with a completely different person from the hot woman with whom he'd gone to bed.

His pride had been stung. He'd been thinking about their day and the ones after that, and she hadn't known how to get rid of him fast enough.

In that moment, of course, the Wentworth-Granville feud had become personal. He'd vowed to end the stalemate between the families, once and for all.

He played to win. It was why he'd engaged in a secret purchase of some prime London real estate, unbeknownst to the Wentworths.

"Be careful, Easterbridge," Hawk said, recalling him from his thoughts. "Even seasoned gamblers have their losses."

Sawyer nodded. "I haven't bested you at poker anytime

lately, but on the other hand, one could argue that just means you're overdue for a dry spell."

Colin quirked his mouth. "I'm happy with the cards that I'm holding at the moment."

Four

Seven months later

*S*oon she'd be free.

Or at least single again—she wasn't sure if she'd ever be free of family obligations and expectations. For one thing, her family still had the expectation that she would marry again—and marry well.

As she steered her rental car up the drive of the private estate, Belinda forced herself to relax.

Nevada was known for granting quick and simple annulments. Fortunately for her, because she and Colin had married right here in Las Vegas, she didn't even have to establish the usual six weeks' residency in Nevada in order to take advantage of the court system.

Colin had kept her on the hook long enough, she'd decided. She'd waited until her June wedding fiasco had faded from everyone's memory. She'd spent months stewing, not wanting more of a scandal but not knowing how to avoid one, either. Now she hoped to quietly have her marriage to Colin dissolved.

She was going for broke trying to get an annulment rather than a divorce. Nevada made it a relatively simple matter to obtain an annulment, unlike New York. With an annulment, it would be as if her marriage had never existed.

Unfortunately, her relationship with Tod had been a casualty of the past several months of her wait-and-see approach. They'd had a parting of the ways, and she could hardly blame him. Who wanted to wait around while his fiancée continued to be married to another man?

She'd gone scouring for a work assignment in Nevada so she could obtain her annulment without tipping anyone off as to her real purpose. Fortunately, something had fallen into her lap. An anonymous collector wished to have his private collection of French impressionist art appraised.

She'd do her work, and in the meantime, she already had a meeting scheduled with a lawyer tomorrow to see about the paperwork for her annulment.

She emerged from her car in front of an impressive Spanish-style hacienda and breathed in the warm air. She looked around the drive, which was alive with the color of cactus flowers. The weather in this suburb of Las Vegas was mild and lovely in March—a contrast to what she was used to in New York or back home in England. Just a slight breeze caressed her arms, which were bare in the sleeveless wheat-colored belted dress that she wore.

She'd been told that the mansion was more of an investment property than anything else and that its owner resided elsewhere. Still, it seemed to be very well maintained. Clearly the owner was someone willing to invest plenty of time and effort in his property.

She looked around. There were no other vehicles visible in the drive, but she had been told that a small staff made sure that the estate ran properly.

Within moments, however, the housekeeper with whom she had spoken through the intercom at the front gate opened the arched aged-wood front door. The middle-aged woman greeted her with a smile and ushered her inside.

After declining any refreshment, Belinda let the housekeeper give her a short tour of the lower level of the house. As an art appraiser, she often found it helpful to see how clients lived generally. The rooms here were large and tastefully decorated but devoid of personal memorabilia—like a staged photo shoot for a home-furnishings catalog. She supposed she shouldn't be surprised, because the mansion was just an investment property.

After a quarter of an hour, she followed the older woman upstairs to what she was told functioned more or less as the art gallery.

When the housekeeper pulled open the double doors, Belinda stepped inside the vast room—and immediately sucked in a breath.

She identified a Monet, a Renoir and a Degas. They were lesser known works, of course, since the most famous ones hung in museums around the world. Still, from her point of view as an art expert, there was no such thing as an obscure Renoir.

More importantly, she recognized the paintings as works that had come to auction in the past few years— *her auctions*. The auctions she'd organized had gone so well as to earn her a promotion at Lansing's.

She'd wondered then whom the mysterious buyer or buyers had been. In her line of work, it wasn't unusual for a buyer to wish to remain unknown, sometimes using a business entity through which to make purchases. But whoever the owner was, Belinda had envied him or her even then.

The paintings were beautiful—dappled, romantic works of art. She wished *she* had had the money to purchase them. She admired the sensibility of the owner and the good sense shown in the way of the paintings' display.

The room was a mini-museum. It was large, had white walls and sported temperature control. The few pieces of furniture were arranged so that no matter where one sat, one had an excellent view of the paintings on the walls.

The housekeeper gave her a smile and then a polite nod. "I'll leave you to your work."

Belinda glanced at the older woman, who looked indulgent at how overwhelmed she was. "Thank you."

After the housekeeper departed, Belinda walked to the center of the room. She stood there for a moment, turning first to the Renoir and then to the Monet. She sat down on a nearby chair for further contemplation.

She was delighted that the paintings had found a place together. They were some of those she'd loved best among those that she'd been fortunate enough to have cross her desk. She'd performed her role well and sold them to the highest bidders for excellent prices. She had scattered them far and wide—or so she thought.

But now she could have her cake and eat it, too—sort of. They were all here.

The Monet was of a man and women in close conversation against a green landscape. The Renoir was a couple dancing in a close embrace. And the Degas was a ballerina figure in pirouette.

After minutes had ticked by, she stood up and moved to the Renoir to inspect it more closely.

The brushstrokes were, of course, exactly as she remembered them.

She heard the door of the room open, and before she could turn around, a voice reached her.

"I believe they're worth more than I paid for them."

The tone was dry, amused...and familiar.

She froze, and then a second later as she pivoted, her eyes collided with the Marquess of Easterbridge's.

"You."

Colin's lips tilted upward. "I believe the correct term is husband."

"How did you get in here?" she demanded.

He looked amused. "I own this house."

Belinda stared at him, her mind reeling as she tried to absorb his words.

Colin looked fit and healthy, and he dressed like an aristocrat at play. He wore a white shirt with rolled cuffs and dark trousers with a thin belt. She assumed they were all ordered from a Savile Row tailor that the Granvilles had patronized for generations.

As usual, Colin was cool and self-possessed. There wasn't a trace of the cat who ate the canary, though she supposed he was entitled to the feeling right now.

"Returning to the scene of the crime?" she asked, desperate to mask how he had rattled her.

She wouldn't give him the satisfaction of immediately launching into an angry polemic about how he had tricked and cornered her.

His eyes gleamed. "The wedding, you mean? It's our third anniversary, you know."

She tossed her hair and feigned indifference. "Really? I didn't recall. All I'm waiting for is the chance to celebrate our annulment."

Colin sauntered farther into the room. "So that's why you're back in Las Vegas?"

"Whether you cooperate or not," she stated unequivocally.

Colin continued to look unperturbed. In her dreams, he wouldn't respond to the service of annulment papers on him. There'd be an uncontested dissolution of their marriage. Of course, in her dreams, she also regularly had a disturbing replay of their passionate night in Vegas.

He gestured around them. "I hope you enjoy examining these works of art."

She regarded him suspiciously. "What are you up to?"

He gave her a small smile. "Isn't it obvious?"

"You lured me here."

"On the contrary, you came willingly in order to obtain an annulment." He regarded her. "I will admit to guessing that you'd probably make your way back to Vegas sooner or later. I thought I'd make the trip worth your while."

"And so you're having some impressionist art work appraised?" she mocked. "Are you planning to sell them?"

Despite herself, she felt sad that he might sell and split up these beautiful paintings. If only she had the means to offer to buy them herself.

Colin tilted his head. "No, I have no intention of selling. At the moment, I'm far more interested in cultivating my investments."

She felt palpable relief, even though she told herself again that what he did, or didn't do, was of no matter to her. "You recently bought these paintings. Why would you want them appraised? There hasn't been enough time for any significant appreciation." She pursued her lips. "They are authentic, you know. I can personally vouch for it."

"Ah, authenticity," he murmured. "It's what I look for."

She shifted, aware that he might be talking about something other than the paintings.

Colin tilted his head. "As I said, I wanted confirmation

that I paid a good price. Like most of my investments, I think they're worth more than I bought them for—at least, now."

Again, Belinda experienced the uncomfortable feeling that there was a subtext to his words that she didn't wholly understand.

"You can't put a precise number on art, though many people try to," she responded. "Beauty is in the eye of the beholder after all."

"So I've understood," he responded, his tone soft.

She watched him look her over, down to the tips of her toes. His gaze started with her face—she only wore light makeup—traveled down to her dress, lingered at her bust and ended with her peep-toe floral-print sandals.

She felt the weight of that look on her breasts and at the juncture of her thighs, even before it made her strangely unstable on her legs.

It was an appreciative look—and enough to belatedly bring out her combative instinct.

"Why are you doing this?" It was time to drop all pretense.

"Perhaps I would like to lay claim to being the one who finally buried the Wentworth-Granville feud." To his credit, he didn't pretend to misunderstand her meaning, but his gaze remained enigmatic.

"If you want to end this feuding between *us,* all you have to do is sign the dissolution papers."

"Hardly any valor to lay claim to in that—it's far too passive."

"You could always divorce me on the grounds of adultery," she suggested hopefully.

She tossed out the rude comment as a gambit and then regretted it when Colin looked keen and possessive.

"Yours or mine?" he asked.

"Mine, of course."

"You're a terrible liar."

"I don't know what you mean."

"Of course you do. You never slept with Dillingham."

His audacity took her breath away.

"Really," she answered with scorn. "And how would you know that? Confident that you ruined me for any other man?"

His smile was deceptively slow and mild. "No, but a marriage contracted to save the family farm is rarely full of passion."

Belinda sucked in a breath.

"And then there's the fact that you had sex with me here in Vegas three years ago only after we were married. What did you say you'd come to understand? You were looking for a man who played for keeps? I guessed that you were likewise making Tod wait."

Belinda realized she was chewing on her bottom lip and abruptly stopped—to anyone who knew her well, her habit was a giveaway that she was nervous. Three years ago, she'd still been smarting from being tossed aside by a boyfriend.

"Except I ruined matters for you with Dillingham, didn't I?" Colin continued. "And now, in desperation, Uncle Hugh has taken matters into his own hands. I bet you had no idea the Wentworth financial affairs were quite so desperate."

Her eyes widened. "What do you mean?"

She should have figured that Colin had an ace up his sleeve. After all, she'd seen his successful streak at the poker tables three years ago. And she knew from his real-estate holdings that he had an uncanny ability with numbers and investing.

"Have you spoken with your uncle lately?" he countered.

"No." Belinda searched her brain. "What's wrong with Uncle Hugh?"

"Nothing, but he has given up his Mayfair town house."

Belinda knew her uncle moved around on a regular basis. "There's nothing unusual—"

"Permanently."

Belinda stilled. "Why would he do that?"

"Because the Mayfair town house now belongs to me."

Belinda shook her head. "That's impossible."

Just a few months ago, she'd been at the Mayfair address that had belonged to the Wentworth family for generations. True, her uncle had seemed preoccupied and worried, but she'd never imagined—

"On the contrary, you'll find the deed has been properly recorded…unlike our annulment. Your uncle may still reside there on his estates, but it's at my discretion."

Belinda looked at him with stupefaction. "Why in the world would Uncle Hugh sell the town house to you? You're the last person in the world to whom he'd sell."

"Simple," Colin responded in a dry tone. "He wasn't aware I was the ultimate buyer. The town house was sold to one of my companies. Presumably he didn't know I was the principal shareholder. I imagine he thought he was selling to one of those newly minted Russian oligarchs who prize privacy as well as London real estate."

She stared at Colin in astonishment. It couldn't be…

Colin shrugged. "It was a quick sale for an agreeable price. Your uncle was apparently looking for a quick infusion of cash."

"What does that have to do with me?" she demanded defiantly.

"I also already owned the larger of the two Berkshire estates."

Belinda's shoulders lowered. The Wentworth family

had, somewhat unusually, two estates in Berkshire. The smaller of the two was of more recent origin, having come into the family through the marriage of her great-great-grandmother. The larger—which Colin apparently now owned, if his claims were to be believed—had been in the family since the days of Edward III. Downlands, as it was called, bordered Granville land, and had been the subject of a prolonged property-line dispute with Colin's family in the nineteenth century.

Belinda's head buzzed. She had no responsibility for the Wentworth estates, she told herself. After all, she had her life in New York as an art dealer. She was far from the family fray—or was she?

"I suppose you acquired the Berkshire estate through a similar anonymous purchase? The privately held company that you used for the transaction wouldn't be LG Management, would it?" She named the mysterious company that she had been told owned the Las Vegas hacienda that they were in.

Colin inclined his head. "LG Management, yes." He quirked his lips. "Lord Granville Management."

Belinda's eyes narrowed. "How clever of you."

"I'm glad you think so."

Her mind raced even more. How was it possible that the family holdings had been so diminished and she had been unaware of it? Was the family's financial situation that dire?

"How did you pay for your lavish wedding to Tod?" Colin asked, seemingly reading her mind.

Belinda started guiltily. "It's none of your business."

Colin thrust his hands in his pockets. "I imagine that in the customary way the Dillinghams bore some of the cost, but as far as the Wentworth share, I can't imagine that you shouldered the entire burden."

The truth was that she had paid for a portion of her wedding. But when Uncle Hugh and her mother had insisted on a lavish affair, she'd given in—on the condition that they bear the additional expense.

"I imagine that Hugh saw your nuptials as Napoleon's escape from Elba," Colin said, connecting the dots for her. "It was his last, desperate gamble to save the family legacy through a fresh infusion of cash from the Dillinghams. Unfortunately, it instead became his Waterloo."

She stared at Colin in disbelief. It was inconceivable that a Granville owned Wentworth land now. But then again, she imagined that some people found it hard to comprehend that a Wentworth—namely, her—was married to a Granville.

But all was not lost, she told herself.

"Even if you own both properties," she countered, "as your wife, I have a claim to them. We are married, after all."

She'd learned *something* from consulting a matrimonial lawyer.

Colin's eyes gleamed with reluctant admiration. "Yes, but only to half the property at most, in all likelihood. And at best, you might be able to get a legal accounting, but then you'd only be entitled to a portion of the cash value from the sale of the estates to a third party."

The rat. Colin would rigorously litigate. She should have known better than to try to best Colin at his own game. Business moguls like him kept schools of corporate lawyers well-fed.

"What about the property that you acquired through your business during our nonmarriage?" she challenged. "Wouldn't that be considered marital property subject to division in a divorce? We don't have a prenuptial agreement."

"Since our marriage has been brief and defunct from day one—" he didn't say thanks to you, though Belinda felt the words as an accusation "—it's unlikely that a court would view those as up for grabs. In any case, I assume your first priority would be trying to get back the Wentworth estate."

Belinda tried to keep the defeat out of her shoulders, because he was right.

"It seems we're at an impasse."

"You've obviously given this thought," she accused.

"Quite, but then three years is a long time to ruminate... about having a wife without conjugal rights."

Belinda felt the flush crawl up her face. "What makes you think I give a fig for what happens to some old buildings and parcels of land an ocean away?"

"Oh, you do," he returned silkily. "The Mayfair town house and the Berkshire estate are where you spent your childhood."

Belinda bit her bottom lip.

"I only observed you from afar," Colin added mockingly, "but I was aware enough of your comings and goings to understand that much."

He was right, damn him.

She recalled running through the halls of the Mayfair town house when she was four or five, and later, learning to ride a horse on the Berkshire estate. And then there had been the innumerable dinner parties. She'd watched her mother get ready for them by donning an expensive gown and selecting the jewels from the family safe. When she was still an adolescent, she'd been invited to join those dinner parties. It was where she'd first met artists of national and international importance and learned the love of art that she'd turned into a career.

Still, she knew enough not to give away too much. "What do you want?"

"I want the woman I married. The one who made decisions for herself, instead of following in her family's footsteps. For a wife like that, I might be willing to come to some sort of compromise about the disposal of my properties."

"I'm not into rebellion enough to be your wife."

"Oh, you're more of a rebel than you think," Colin returned smoothly, stepping closer.

Belinda lifted her eyebrows in mock inquiry.

"One can even say your move to New York, distancing yourself from the other Wentworths, was a small act of rebellion."

She felt strangely exposed.

"It's your choice," Colin said. "You can choose to be a Princess Leia or a Han Solo. You can choose to be a stick-in-the-mud and annul our marriage for another safe and family-approved husband, or you can be someone who lives life according to her own terms. Which is it going to be?"

"Frankly, it's like being offered a bargain by Darth Vader," she tossed back, covering her sudden confusion.

Colin's eyes crinkled, and then he laughed.

Belinda swallowed. Despite her flippant response, Colin's words hit close to home. But then, what did he know of her life? She wasn't a stick-in-the-mud, damn it. She was just responsible.

This conversation was enough to make a girl long for some shopping therapy.

"What's in this for you?" she asked.

"I told you. I'm cultivating an investment."

She fought the urge to stamp her foot in frustration. "I don't know what that means."

"Does it matter?" he retorted. "Your side of the game is clear. You can do as your family dictates and end our marriage, but that may leave the Wentworth heritage solely in my hands. Is that what you want?"

What she wanted? She had no idea, not anymore. There was too much at stake, and he was far too attractive, standing so close to her, looking so powerful and in control.

"The other option is better," he tempted. "By staying married to me, you can both rebel and play the role of dutiful daughter or niece at the same time. It's rare that such an opportunity presents itself."

She tried to wrap her mind around what he was saying.

"Stay married to me, and you can move these paintings to Downlands."

"To Downlands?" she challenged, licking suddenly dry lips. "Downlands is no longer mine."

"It could be solely yours," Colin countered, his voice low and smooth, "if we remain married. I'll sign that contract."

She wasn't ready for this. She needed time to process... think...

But Colin wasn't giving her time or space. He stepped closer, within touching distance.

She felt a sizzle skate along her nerve endings.

His hair was short and silky, like mink, and his eyes were dark and gave nothing away. She noticed the tiny crinkles at the corners of his eyes that had grown infinitesimally more pronounced from three years ago.

She shifted her gaze downward, over the hard planes of his cheekbones and nose, to his mouth. For a hard man, he had soft lips.

As she well knew. On their wedding night, he'd kissed every inch of her, doing a leisurely survey, as she had lain on black satin sheets, the petals from the roses that he'd hastily procured for their ceremony haphazardly scattered around them.

He'd used the petals to tickle and arouse her until she'd moaned and writhed, practically panting for him to take her.

He'd been equally affected. His heart had beat hard and fast, and when he'd slid inside her, there hadn't been a moment's doubt about how much he wanted her.

It had been the most decadent thing she'd ever done in her life.

Colin's lips moved. "You look practically slumberous."

She jerked her gaze upward and then felt red-hot heat stain her cheeks.

He looked amused but intent. "What were you thinking about? Remembering the last time we were in Vegas?"

Remember? She could feel him in every pore, like an airy caress.

"It was a mistake," she said automatically.

"How do you know?" he responded. "You refuse to test the proposition."

"I don't need to touch fire again to know I'll get burned."

She realized instantly that her analogy was off, because his eyes kindled.

"Interesting choice of words," he murmured. "Is that what we were? Did we go up in smoke?"

"I didn't say—"

He rested his finger against her lips, stopping her words. They both went still, searching each other's eyes.

He lowered his hand only to trail his finger down her chin and then her throat, in a light caress.

He slid his hand to cup the side of her neck, and his thumb found and came to rest on her pulse.

The rapid beat of her heart was a giveaway as to how affected she was, and they both knew it.

"It was good, wasn't it?" he asked, rubbing soothingly over her rapid pulse. "The best sex ever."

She swallowed, and her lips parted. She had tried not to think about it, but yes, it had been the most sensational night of her life.

"Should I feel flattered?" she challenged.

He laughed. "Maybe lucky is more like it, since similar nights can be yours for free."

"Everything has a price."

"I'm willing to keep paying."

"And what will *I* have to pay?"

"Next to nothing compared to what you'll receive… and what we can create together. What we have created together, remember?"

She sucked in a breath. "It was Vegas. It makes you do crazy things."

"We're back here, breathing the same air. And it's our anniversary."

Dear Lord. "Our families are enemies. It was forbidden sex, nothing more."

"We're married. I'm legally yours and you're legally mine."

"Only because you haven't fought fair."

"You said that you wanted a man who played for keeps, because you'd been burned before. Yet you threw me back the next morning."

"So what is it you want now, revenge sex?"

He smiled enigmatically. "Is that going to be your excuse if it's just as explosive?"

She started to turn her head to the side, but his mouth came down on hers before her denial was complete.

Three years. Three years she'd lived with the memory

of what it was like to kiss and be possessed by Colin Granville, Marquess of Easterbridge.

In one moment, however, the memory was washed away by an even more vivid reality.

If Colin had been demanding, she might have had a better chance of resisting him. But he kissed her languidly, as if he was enjoying a sweet drink and had all the time in the world.

He tasted minty and warm. He slid his tongue into her mouth and coaxed her into deepening the kiss.

Belinda felt every sensation as if she was doing tequila shots without the lime. It was heady, and there was no respite.

Colin slid his hand to her rear end, bringing her flush up against his undeniable arousal, and his other hand slid around her back, molding her to him.

Belinda could feel everything through the thin fabric of her matte jersey dress. She became aware of her nipples jutting and pressing into the unyielding wall of his chest.

She'd been hoping her memories were exaggerated, but Colin lived up to billing and more.

Being in his arms was an intoxicating mix of the dangerous—as if she was walking on a precipice and he was tempting her into unknown and risky territory—and the comforting. He was solid and capable and made her feel oddly free, as if with him, at least, she could finally and truly be herself.

Strange. She shouldn't feel as if he was someone to whom she might shift her burden. He was a Granville, she reminded herself, and she still wasn't sure what game he was playing. And it didn't help that she'd just confirmed she had a visceral sexual reaction to him.

She stilled and then pulled away.

Colin let her go reluctantly.

They stared at each other, both breathing deeply.

Colin's eyes glittered, but then he gained mastery of himself and banked the fires.

Belinda could only imagine what she looked like. Her lips tingled from his kiss, and she fought a sudden unsettling urge to slip back into his arms for more.

She started to raise her hand to her lips, belatedly realized Colin caught the movement and then abruptly stopped herself.

She bent and grabbed her purse, then turned on her heel and hurried to the door.

She didn't care that she was fleeing—and he was letting her.

He spoke behind her. "The paintings—"

"The price is too high."

Five

Belinda glanced around the elegantly appointed Mayfair town house. Her visit was like her last…with one important difference.

The town house no longer belonged to the Wentworths, as it had for generations, but was merely on loan. Despite the illusion of permanence afforded by the decor of family antiques, everything was ephemeral.

Her uncle continued to reside here at the Marquess of Easterbridge's pleasure. Uncle Hugh could have the heirloom Persian rug pulled out from under him at any moment.

"Tell me it isn't true."

She said the words without preamble after appearing unannounced in the library. She knew this conversation was too important to have over the phone. She'd arranged a flight to London as soon as she could, right after flying back to New York from Vegas without making any progress on an annulment.

Uncle Hugh regarded her from behind his desk. "Whatever are you talking about, my dear?" He shook his head. "I didn't even know you were in London. You do lead the peripatetic existence these days, don't you?"

"I just arrived this morning." Belinda glanced around her. "Tell me you did not sell this house."

After a moment, Uncle Hugh visibly crumbled. "How did you find out?"

"Does it matter?" she responded.

After she'd taken off from the hacienda, she'd considered that Colin might call her uncle himself to mention their meeting in Vegas and to reveal himself as the cloaked buyer. She'd dreaded that he'd go public with the news. But judging from her uncle's reaction, he hadn't done anything—so far.

Upon reflection, she realized that she should have known Colin would leave it to her to make the shocking revelation to her uncle that his buyer was the Marquess of Easterbridge. *Of course.*

Still, she wondered what it signified. Did Colin intend to derive every satisfaction from vanquishing her uncle, including having Belinda confront her relative, or did he think it was more merciful for her to deliver the news rather than for him to reveal it himself?

"I was assured of discretion," Uncle Hugh said, his tone defensive. "I am continuing to live here and at the estate in Berkshire, and nobody needs to be the wiser about the change in ownership."

Belinda looked at him with a sinking heart. "Assured of discretion for how long and by whom? The Russian billionaire to whom you thought you sold the property for investment purposes?"

Uncle Hugh nodded. "The agreement was for me to

continue to live here for years." He paused. "How did you find out? If you know, then—"

"You fell into a trap. A layer of corporate entities obscured his identity, but the buyer is none other than the Marquess of Easterbridge."

Uncle Hugh looked flabbergasted and then bowed his head and clasped his forehead with his hand.

"Why didn't you tell me the family finances were so dire?" Belinda demanded.

"There's nothing you could have done."

"How did we reach this pass?"

She had a right to know, especially since she was on the spot for getting them out of this quagmire. At least, the smaller of the Berkshire estates remained in Wentworth hands, so her family would never be completely without a home, but their identity was tied up in the properties that they no longer owned.

Her uncle glanced up and shook his head, his look beseeching. "Our financial investments have not done well in the past few years. There are also family members with significant allowances. Your mother..."

Neither of them needed to say more. Belinda was well aware of her mother's lavish lifestyle. She made no mention, however, of Uncle Hugh's own expensive tastes. Of course, her uncle would not view them as such. After all, what was the cost of a bespoke suit to one who had worn them for all his adult life?

As for herself, Belinda supplemented her modest salary at Lansing's with a small trust fund that her grandparents and father had left her, so she had not needed to draw an allowance. If she had known the specifics, however, she would have gladly turned over her trust fund to save the family ship from sinking. At the same time, she doubted it would have done much good aside from buying them a small amount of time.

Belinda studied her uncle. He'd always loomed large in her life—someone to look up to. She'd grown up under his roof. But now he appeared diminished by more than merely his years. The shoe was on the other foot now, and Belinda felt uncomfortably like she was chastising a child.

Uncle Hugh bent his head. "It's all ruined."

"Not quite."

She knew what ruin felt like—her wedding day had been a disaster—so her heart went out to her uncle. At the same time, she stopped herself from pointing out that while she had been castigated for marrying a Granville, Uncle Hugh had sold the family estates to one, albeit inadvertently. Who had committed the greater transgression?

Her uncle glanced up. "What do you mean?"

"I mean Colin is reluctant to grant me a divorce, though he ultimately may not have a choice." Nothing was ever quite as lost as one believed, she was discovering.

Uncle Hugh brightened. "We may have some leverage."

"I knew you'd think so," she commented drily.

"Yes, yes." Her uncle looked more animated by the second. "You must stay married to him."

Belinda bit her lip. Stay married to Colin? She'd avoided dwelling on the possibility since leaving Vegas.

Uncle Hugh sat up straighter. "Tell him that you'll stay married on condition of his signing over the properties to you."

"What?" she asked, sliding into a seat because she didn't like the direction this conversation was taking. "What possible motivation would he have for doing so? He'd likely think I'd divorce him as soon as I had the deeds to the properties, and he'd be right!"

"Then negotiate," her uncle replied, setting his hands on his desk. "Have him turn over the properties one by one."

Belinda's stomach felt as if it were a roller coaster. "A postnuptial agreement?"

"Exactly." Her uncle nodded. "It's done all the time."

Belinda worried her lip. Why was it up to her to save the family fortunes?

Colin was right—this *was* her chance to be the rebel and the dutiful child all at once. But she never would have dreamed that Uncle Hugh would latch on to the idea with such enthusiasm. This is the most her family had ever asked of her. It was all preposterous and outrageous. Yet she found herself considering it.

"Why would Colin want to stay married to me?" she rejoined.

Her uncle looked at her keenly. "Now there's a question for the marquess. You're an attractive girl. And perhaps he wants to save face with society. After all, you did almost marry another man while you remained his wife. If you and the marquess live as man and wife for a period of time, it'll stamp out the taint."

Belinda felt her shoulders slump. She didn't believe Colin cared a fig about society—after all, *he* was the one who had generated a scandal by interrupting her wedding. But soothing the blow to his pride? Yes, *that* she could believe. She had rejected Colin after their Vegas wedding. She'd fled, fearful of what she'd done, and had beat a hasty retreat down the reckless path she'd traveled in one night.

If she had instigated Colin's drive for revenge, wasn't she responsible for rectifying the fallout?

The thought swept through Belinda's mind. Her world

was no longer a neat painting but one streaked with bold and unexpected new colors.

She was no longer faced with the relatively simple matter of dissolving her marriage to Colin. The Wentworth heritage was in Granville hands. And the responsible streak in her wouldn't let her walk away without making an effort to save it, especially if she'd had a hand in bringing about the current situation.

Still, even if she was responsible, could she play a high-stakes game with a seasoned gambler?

Her cell phone buzzed, interrupting her thoughts, and she fished it out of her handbag to glance down at a text message.

Meet @ Halstead—DH

Belinda's mind churned. The message could be interpreted as a summons, a request or a question. Halstead Hall was the family seat in Berkshire of the Marquess of Easterbridge. Though Belinda didn't recognize the phone number, there was no mistaking whom the text was from. Colin had cleverly signed himself as *DH—darling husband* in text parlance.

There was one way to find out the answer to the question of whether she was up to the task of saving the Wentworth family fortune.

Her campaign would be if not exactly snatching victory from the jaws of disaster then at least surviving to fight another day.

"I'll remain married to you."

Belinda felt like a defeated army general being summoned for the signing of a peace treaty, all of whose terms had been dictated by the other side. Her job was to salvage what she could.

In a nod to the nippy March weather, her armor was a cowl-neck sweaterdress and knee-high boots.

Colin stood beside the fireplace in a drawing room of Halstead Hall. He wore a knit pullover over wool trousers—typical English country-gentleman attire.

He raised an eyebrow.

"I have certain conditions, however," she said from a few feet away, having declined a seat.

She tried not to look around, because she feared she might be daunted. She'd never been inside Halstead Hall before, but of course she was familiar with the house and surrounding estate. Together they formed a Berkshire landmark, and she'd grown up literally next door.

The house was an immense monolith with a beauty all its own. It had been started in the sixteenth century and added onto ever since. There were enough turrets, arched entries and paned windows to impress the most discerning *cognoscenti,* let alone the typical tourist.

Belinda had found it almost comical to be greeted at the door by the housekeeper and addressed as Lady Granville. Obviously, Colin had informed his staff about what to expect after she'd texted him back and accepted his invitation to meet—or perhaps, more accurately, set down arms—at Halstead Hall. To her credit, the housekeeper had acted as if Belinda's arrival at the front door was already an everyday occurrence.

Belinda knew she had taken on quite a bit by meeting Easterbridge in his bastion. But if nothing else, their recent encounters had shown her that negotiations would take place on his terms. The ball was, quite literally, in his court.

If the outside of Halstead Hall was an impressive testament to centuries of wealth and power, then the inside bore witness to the current occupant's money and prestige. Everything had been updated for modern comfort but was still in keeping with the house's history and majesty. The whole vast interior had central heat, twenty-first century plumbing and insulation and barely a creaky floorboard.

There were finely wrought plaster ceilings, and antique furniture and marble busts. She recognized paintings from Rubens and Gainsborough, among others.

It was all in depressing contrast to the Wentworth properties. She'd grown up with her great-grandmother's Victorian china, but not wealth of the caliber that existed at Halstead Hall. She knew that Downlands needed a long-overdue modernization of its plumbing and heating, and the Mayfair town house required a new roof.

"Of course you have conditions," Colin said smoothly. "Would one of those be having a wedding ceremony that does not involve a Vegas chapel?"

"No, definitely not." She didn't appreciate his sardonic humor. It was bad enough that she had come back to him with proverbial hat in hand. "I said I'd stay married to you—not that I'd marry you again."

She'd already survived an elopement and a wedding. She didn't want to push her luck. Because let's face it, she and the altar had a love-hate relationship.

His reaction wasn't what she'd anticipated. It was cool and calculating, despite a certain intensity in his gaze.

"There's a difference?" he asked mockingly.

"Of course," she replied. "Can you imagine what our two families would do if they had to sit across a church aisle from each other?"

"Make peace and attribute it to divine intervention?" he quipped.

"Quite the opposite, I'm sure."

"It might make for a good show."

"I'd rather take my chances with an Elvis impersonator."

"You almost did."

"Don't remind me." She'd declined—just barely—the offer of an Elvis wannabe to witness her elopement.

"So what are your conditions?"

"I want you to sign over the Wentworth properties to my name."

"Ah." Colin's eyes gleamed, as if he'd been expecting her demand.

Belinda raised her chin. "It's a fair bargain. After all, they are what is keeping this marriage alive."

Colin tilted his head. "Considering how weak your bargaining position is, it's an impressive demand. After all, your only bargaining chip is to threaten to dissolve our marriage, but then you wouldn't necessarily wind up with the Wentworth estates anyway."

Belinda felt her face heat but stood her ground.

She'd learned a few things during her years as an art specialist. One of them was to start bargaining by asking for more than one could possibly hope to get. It was up to him to make a counteroffer.

"And more than that," Colin continued, "what assurance do I receive that you won't go running off to Vegas for a dissolution the moment that I do sign the properties over to you?"

"You have my pledge."

Colin laughed. "You're delectable, but you are a Wentworth."

Belinda ignored how her pulse skittered and skated over the word *delectable*. "And you're a Granville."

"It does come down to that, doesn't it?"

She shot him a distinctly unamused look.

"I'll suggest a compromise."

"Oh?" *Here it comes.*

"Yes," he continued. "I'll sign the properties over to you one by one on a schedule. The longer we're married, the more you receive if we divorce."

Belinda felt a sense of relief wash over her. Colin was suggesting exactly what her uncle had in London three days ago.

Still, it rankled that the two men had pigeonholed her—and that they thought alike.

She had to admit, however, that the plan made a crazy sort of sense. After all, given her preference, she'd get an annulment or divorce tomorrow, while Colin wouldn't. This way, they got a marriage for some indefinite duration—not for forever, but on the other hand, not over tomorrow.

"One property every six months," she said, forcing herself to put down the demand without blinking.

To her surprise, Colin didn't blink, either. But then, she thought, he was a seasoned gambler.

Finally, he lifted the side of his mouth. "You're a good negotiator."

"I appraise and auction artwork for a living."

He inclined his head. "We're alike in that way, I suppose. We're both skilled in the art of the deal."

She didn't want to discover she had one more thing in common with him. They already had too much.

"You haven't said whether you agree to my terms," she reminded him.

He tilted his head. "One year for each, and at the end of two, both the Mayfair town house and the Berkshire estate are yours."

She opened her mouth to protest. *Two years?*

And yet, she acknowledged, it was a rather fair offer.

Two years would still leave her plenty of time to get on with her life after her marriage was officially over.

"Agreed." Still, she perversely pushed the envelope. "And what's to prevent me from divorcing you at the end?"

Colin smiled enigmatically. "Perhaps I'm banking on the fact that you won't want to."

He surprised her by departing from the script that she'd been preparing for ever since her conversation with her uncle. He was supposed to say that he was trying to repair the blow to his ego and remove the taint on his name. She, in return, was supposed to be in the position of disdaining his shallow motives.

Instead, his bravado took her breath away.

"The position of marchioness comes with benefits," he said in a low, seductive voice. "Estates, cars, travel…"

"I've seen plenty of money and fame. I come across it regularly as part of my job at Lansing's."

He shrugged, easy and self-assured. "What else can I tempt you with?"

"I'm surprised you didn't put yourself at the top of the list," she challenged.

Colin laughed. "Okay, *me.*"

Good Lord. She hadn't done a good job of resisting him for one night three years ago in Vegas. How was she going to erect a wall against him for the long haul?

Colin was suddenly looking at her with a renewed intensity. "It was good, wasn't it? We were good."

"I was out of my mind—"

"With passion, don't deny it."

"I'd had a couple of drinks—"

"One Kamikaze?" he queried.

"The name says it all. And don't forget most of a Sex on the Beach."

He waved away her response. "It was hours earlier."

"They created a nice buzz."

Colin smiled. "It wasn't sex on the beach, but it was close, wasn't it? There was the scent of sun and surf. Then I realized it was you."

She resisted putting her hands over her ears. "Don't remind me!"

She'd never worn that perfume again. It carried too many memories.

She wasn't sure whether to take him seriously. He would say anything to win, except she wasn't quite sure what the endgame was.

"Why are you doing this?" she blurted.

She'd demanded an answer to that question before, but this time it was a metaphorical stamping of the foot.

"Perhaps I enjoy the challenge of going where no Granville has gone before."

"Straight to hell?" she asked sweetly.

Colin laughed.

"One of your villainous ancestors seduced a Wentworth heiress," she reminded him.

"Seduction—is that what she claimed?" he scoffed. "More likely, she had fallen for the handsome lad before her family packed her off to God knows where."

"Of course that story would be the Granville version."

"Sad to say, the poor lad ultimately didn't get a chance to marry her. I've accomplished what no Granville has before."

"It'll be a Pyrrhic victory."

Colin smiled. "I'll be the judge of that."

Belinda felt his words like a caress.

He suddenly straightened and then walked over to a nearby console table.

No doubt the table was an original eighteenth-century piece, Belinda thought with bemusement. The Granville wealth dwarfed the Wentworths' and probably had as well in her ancestors' heyday. She admired now the strength of her forebears in standing up to—some would say, *running afoul of*—the highest-ranking nobility in the vicinity.

Colin slid open a drawer and withdrew a small velvet pouch. Then he crossed to her.

Belinda found herself holding her breath as Colin loosened the pouch by its drawstring and then neatly deposit its contents into the palm of his hand.

She widened her eyes. He held two simple gold bands, one a large plain one with a slight groove at the edges and the other a smaller one etched with a feminine pattern.

They'd picked those rings out together just before their Vegas wedding ceremony.

Colin's gaze met hers, and she felt heat and promise in his look.

Then the side of his mouth teased upward. "To seal our bargain."

Belinda watched with sudden dry mouth as he slipped the bigger band on his finger. Then he slid the empty pouch into one of his pockets.

With slow deliberation, he lifted her hand, his grip sure and firm, and slid the smaller wedding band onto her finger.

Belinda tried to keep her hand steady, fighting a tremor.

She knew what she was doing, she told herself. She was strong and capable.

Still, she sucked in a breath when Colin raised her hand to his lips. He kept his eyes on hers as he very properly blew a kiss right over the back of her hand.

She felt relief—and yes, a twinge of disappointment

that she quickly banished—before Colin surprised her by turning her hand over.

He leisurely kissed first the pad of one finger and then another, and Belinda felt her heart quicken.

When he was done, he closed his eyes and pressed his lips into her palm.

Belinda took short and shallow breaths.

She felt his warm, soft lips like an erotic brand that sent pulsing sensation down to the tips of her toes.

Why, oh why did Colin know so unerringly how to get under her defenses? He certainly lived up to billing as the descendant of conquerors. Whenever she thought she knew what to expect, he caught her off guard.

Yet despite his calm facade, she could tell he was affected, too. He held himself with a leashed stillness and intensity.

He'd take her right here if she agreed.

The thought raced through her mind, and Belinda felt herself melt. She remembered how passionate their night in Vegas had been. The images were emblazoned on her memory in vivid 3-D, though she'd tried hard over the years not to play that particular movie.

Colin opened his eyes and raised his head, and she ran her tongue over her lips.

He watched the action like a bee drawn to pollen. She knew if he kissed her, her lips would certainly feel bee-stung.

He never did anything in half measures, she realized. In that respect, he'd acted true to form in his current take-no-prisoners battle with the Wentworths.

Belinda straightened her spine and extricated her hand from his.

Colin might be an expert at seduction, but he was also

the one who had plotted the ruination of her family for his own nefarious purposes—and she was his pawn. She might allow her uncle to manipulate her for their family's sake, but she would not allow her husband to control her, as well—certainly not now, before their agreement was officially in place.

Colin's lips quirked with dry humor. "We can always select rings that are more to your liking. Garrard has been the Granville family's jewelers for over a century. Naturally, you can also have your pick from the Granville heirlooms."

"These are fine," Belinda responded, curling her fingers into the palm of the hand that he had kissed.

She wanted the reminder of how their relationship had started with a hasty trip to a Vegas chapel. Somehow, she knew she'd need the clue in the weeks and months to come.

"You'll also need a proper engagement ring."

Belinda was glad the sexual tension had eased, but somehow she still felt under siege. "I'm surprised you don't already have one picked out. This meeting has all the markings of a victor arranging to inventory his spoils."

Unconscionably, Colin grinned. "So you see yourself as a spoil of war? Strangely, I find the analogy to Helen of Troy more compelling."

"The face that launched a thousand ships?" she parried. "I doubt you have a thousand warships to launch."

Colin laughed. "I'll have to be more inventive, then."

Belinda became aware of the pounding of her heart.

Colin had been inventive enough already. She really didn't want him to be any more so.

He bent his head to kiss her, and she took a step back.

She felt her heart skitter. "I'll need some time to adjust—"

At that moment, there was a tap on the door to the drawing room, which was followed by a cough as the door opened.

Belinda was grateful for the interruption.

A butler somberly announced, "The Dowager Marchioness of Easterbridge, has arrived, sir."

Six

Colin bit back an oath.

His promising interlude with Belinda had been cut short.

His mother came and went from Halstead Hall at her leisure, but she refused to use twenty-first century technology like email or text messaging to presage her arrival. *Too common,* she'd sniff.

From the look on Belinda's face, Colin could tell she was as surprised and nonplussed as he was by his mother's unexpected arrival—but for different reasons, he was sure.

"Colin, what is the meaning of this?" his mother said as she sailed into the room. "*Dowager?* Kindly instruct your staff that I haven't been relegated…"

The words trailed off as his mother stopped, realized who else was in the room and widened her eyes.

Colin stepped forward.

"May I introduce my wife, Belinda?" he said, neatly sidestepping the issue of titles and surnames.

After all, one was the Marchioness of Easterbridge and the other the Dowager Marchioness of Easterbridge.

One word of difference disguised the vast gulf between the two women.

Colin watched his mother's face turn different shades before she opened and closed her mouth.

He raised his eyebrows. "Belinda is residing here."

Under any other circumstances, it would have been a rather comical statement to make about one's wife, but all three of them knew there was nothing ordinary about this situation. Why pretend otherwise?

"I thought you meant to find a suitable bride," his mother breathed.

Obviously, Colin thought wryly, he wasn't the only one prepared to drop all pretense.

"Belinda is suitable, Mother."

"She's a Wentworth," his mother responded flatly.

"Well, in that regard, you are correct," he quipped. "Belinda chose to keep her maiden name upon our marriage."

Apparently anything could be forgiven these days except a family feud. A divorcée, a single mother and the descendant of coal miners had married the heirs to thrones across Europe, but if there was bad blood and scandal between neighbors, then all bets were off.

"How do you do?" Belinda spoke up.

Colin noticed that she maintained an admirable poise under the circumstances, but he wondered whether her question was tongue in cheek.

It was clear to everyone that the older marchioness was doing exceedingly *unwell* at the moment.

He scanned Belinda's face, but she didn't glance at him. Instead, she kept her gaze fixed on his mother.

"Colin is correct that I did retain my surname," Belinda said. "It should be quite easy to avoid confusion, I think, if you remain Lady Granville, and I am styled as Lady Wentworth."

His mother gave a haughty stare. She was dressed in tweeds, silks and pearls, and her clothes underlined her expression. "Yes, but you would still be the Marchioness of Easterbridge, would you not?"

Colin tried to avoid looking long-suffering. He detested the way some women were able to throw proverbial knives at each other. His mother excelled at it.

"I am sure, Mother," he said, an edge to his voice, "that you will make Belinda feel comfortable. She needs to learn her way around, and our house is vast." He'd put a subtle but noticeable emphasis on the word *our*. This was Belinda's home now, too, and his mother would need to reconcile herself to the reality.

Belinda turned to face him. "My job is in New York. How will I manage to be employed at Lansing's and reside here?"

"Yes, Easterbridge," his mother joined in. "Do tell us, dear."

Colin lifted the side of his mouth. He had somehow managed to shift the conversation so that Belinda and his mother were aligned against him. If he had any idea how he'd done it, he'd pat himself on the back.

He shot Belinda a glance. "You can arrange a transfer to the London office of Lansing's. We can spend our weeksdays in London and retire to Halstead Hall for weekends."

Brilliant. He was satisfied that he'd walked the tightrope—that is, until he saw Belinda's expression.

She turned from him to his mother, a tight smile on her face. "However, a transfer may be difficult to obtain, so I may be based in New York indefinitely." She tossed him a pointed look. "Colin and I haven't yet discussed our living arrangements in depth."

"You will continue to have a career?" his mother asked cryptically.

Belinda kept her smile. "Yes, at least until I am entitled to receive back my family's property under the terms of the postnup."

His mother looked horrified.

Colin was almost amused by Belinda's determination. He'd married no retiring English rose.

He folded his arms. "Are you shocked by the fact that we didn't have a prenuptial agreement, Mother, or by the fact that we're negotiating a postnuptial one?"

"I should have known a Wentworth would be in this for money," his mother sniffed.

"I would toss him back if it weren't for the properties I stand to regain," Belinda said cheerily.

His mother looked pinched. "My son is not a fish."

"Of course not," Belinda replied before he could say anything. "I don't catch fish—or kiss frogs for that matter."

Colin gave her a sardonic look. "Thank you for clarifying the issue."

At least she was willing to allow he wasn't a frog—while refusing to be cast as a money or title hunter.

His mother looked from one to the other of them until her eyes came to rest on him. "I will see you at dinner, Colin."

She turned on her heel and headed to the door. The subtext of her words, of course, was that she intended to rest until this evening and, with any luck, awaken to the realization that this was all a terrible nightmare.

When the door shut, Colin addressed Belinda. "Well, that went rather well."

She shot him an ironic look. "I'm looking forward to dinner."

Dinner was a pained affair.

Colin watched his younger sister, Sophie, concentrate on spearing her food and chewing while she cast the occasional glance around the table.

Sophie was eight years younger than he was and thus more of Belinda's contemporary than his own. His mother had suffered a miscarriage between their two births and then had had difficulty conceiving again.

As was his mother's preference, dinner was a formal affair in the main dining room, though it was only four who were present for the meal.

Still, even the arrangement of the seating had been a fraught affair. One of his aides had come to see him about it before the appointed dinner hour.

He'd instructed that he'd take his usual seat at the head of the table, and Belinda would be seated to his right. Because of Belinda's presence, his mother had been moved to his left and Sophie farther down the table.

Colin glanced at his sister again. He doubted that Sophie minded being away from the fray. And fortunately, there was plenty of spacing between the seats at the long Victorian dining table.

Colin heaved an inward sigh. He had hoped that the spacing would stop the ladies from lobbing dinner rolls at each other, and so far dinner had been a tame affair—*too tame*.

Conversation had been desultory.

His mother was trying to ignore Belinda, and Sophie was a reluctant participant.

Sophie resembled him in coloring, but she'd had more trouble escaping their mother's influence—no doubt partly because she was younger, and his mother had her own hopes for her only daughter.

Colin looked from his sister to Belinda. They should be at least vaguely familiar with each other. After all, they were only a few years apart in age and had grown up in the same social circles.

He cleared his throat. "Sophie, I would have thought you and Belinda were acquainted."

His sister jerked her head up and gave him an alarmed look. Her eyes darted to their mother before returning to him. "I believe that Belinda and I have been at some of the same social functions, but we hardly spoke."

Everyone, of course, knew why.

The friction between the Granvilles and the Wentworths was legendary, and judging from the conversation tonight, it was also in their blood to be unable to communicate.

Colin would not be deterred. "My sister is a graphic designer, Belinda. She's always coming up with new prints inspired by famous artists."

Belinda and Sophie exchanged wary looks.

"Actually, my designs are influenced by *manga,*" Sophie said. "I've visited Japan several times."

"I've been to Japan for Lansing's," Belinda responded.

Sophie nodded…and the conversation lapsed.

Colin firmed his jaw.

He guessed he wouldn't be able to unearth the witty Belinda tonight even if he had professional digging equipment. The same went for Sophie.

His mother was, of course, a lost cause.

No, the only things that glittered about the women

tonight were their clothes and their jewels. Belinda's beaded top caught the light, competing with his mother's five-carat ruby necklace.

He suddenly saw the months stretching ahead of him like a dusty desert road. If his family and Belinda could barely talk then he'd have to keep them away from each other.

He could easily do so, of course. He owned several houses, and Halstead Hall was quite large. But it rankled that he'd have to resort to it.

This should have been a moment to savor because Belinda was his.

She'd set down her weekend bag in a guest suite when she'd arrived earlier today, but in his mind, now that she'd agreed to remain his wife, it was only a matter of time before he seduced her into thinking that heading back to bed with him was a good idea.

He studied his wife. Her dark hair was loose around her shoulders and just caressing the tops of her breasts. Her lips were full and glistening pink, and her profile straight. The soft lines of her cheek and jaw were outlined by the light and shadows of the dining room.

He wanted her.

They had explosive chemistry in bed, and he was looking forward to enjoying it again.

On the other hand, *explosive* could hardly be used to describe dinner.

It was time, he decided, to ignite the fuse on the proverbial bomb.

He cleared his throat, and three pairs of eyes fixed on him.

"Belinda and I have been invited to the Duke of Hawkshire's wedding to Pia Lumley," he said. "It will be our first public outing as a couple."

Aside, of course, to their literal outing as man and wife at the Wentworth-Dillingham near-miss of a wedding last year, he added silently.

His words rang out like the peal of cathedral bells—though Hawk and Pia were in actuality getting married in a local parish.

Belinda's eyes widened.

Colin could tell it hadn't occurred to her that Pia and Hawk's wedding was next week, and now that she'd agreed to their bargain, they'd be attending together as husband and wife.

His mother, on the other hand, looked aghast.

He guessed she was thinking that next week didn't give her enough time to change his mind or do damage control.

Colin took a last bite of his food, satisfied that he'd taken control of matters.

"By God, you've done it." Uncle Hugh smiled, slapped his knee and then grasped the arm of his leather chair.

Belinda regarded her uncle from where she was sitting on the sofa and had to agree. On the other hand, she and Uncle Hugh almost certainly had different ideas about what his words connoted.

"I hope you're satisfied." The words were a strange echo of the ones that she'd slapped Colin with.

She was back in Uncle Hugh's Mayfair town house after a night at Halstead Hall.

Except, of course, it wasn't her uncle's town house any longer.

Belinda glanced around the sitting room. Her uncle was looking several shades more robust than he had mere days ago, when he'd declared that all was lost. Her mother was as elegant as ever as she sat sipping tea next to Belinda on the sofa. On the surface, there was nothing to distinguish this gathering from hundreds that they'd had in this house before.

But now Belinda *knew* Colin owned these walls.

The town house was furnished with a few antiques but certainly nothing that would impress a marquess used to even grander quarters. Without the family history here that the Wentworths had, what possible use could Colin have for this house?

I intend to make a conquest of the Wentworths once and for all.

Colin's words had become more of a reality than she could possibly have predicted.

When she'd arrived at Halstead Hall two days ago to meet with Colin, she'd immediately been shown to a guest suite, and it had been easy to avoid Colin with the interference of his mother and his sister in the house.

The morning after the stilted family dinner, she'd made her excuses and departed for London and eventually New York to settle her affairs and attend to business, particularly now that she knew she'd be spending more time in England for the foreseeable future.

Colin hadn't appeared happy about her departure, but if he sensed that her work wasn't as pressing as she made it seem, he'd said nothing. Besides, she knew he had his own business matters to attend to.

He seemed content to bide his time, but she knew he was intent on seducing her. They were engaged in a game of cat and mouse, really.

Recalling Belinda back from her thoughts, her mother set down her cup and saucer on a nearby table. "When I asked how you planned to quell the scandal *du jour,* I had no idea that you would do so by staying married to Easterbridge."

"What did you expect me to do, Mother?" Belinda asked.

She'd always felt as if she had a damned-if-you-do, damned-if-you-don't relationship with her mother.

She'd expected her mother to be overjoyed. Uncle Hugh certainly was. But then, her uncle was a lot closer to the family's bills and financial statements than her mother. He was the gatekeeper, while the idea of being financially responsible was one her mother had never grasped.

Her mother sighed. "What will your life be like?"

What, indeed. Belinda had asked herself the same question numerous times since agreeing to remain married to Colin.

She was having a hard time seeing what their marriage would be like. Perhaps, like most couples, they'd have to make things up as they went along.

Belinda bit her lip. What if she became pregnant with Colin's child?

She could only imagine what their two families would think about the joining of their bloodlines and what kind of life their child would have caught between the feuding families.

Belinda gave a slight shake of her head. No, she and Colin had an agreement, and at the end, they would go their separate ways. Implicit in that understanding was the fact that they would plan not to have children.

She was thirty-three. Even if Colin turned the property over to her in two years, she'd be thirty-five and still have some time ahead of her.

She recalled Colin's words when she'd asked what would prevent her from obtaining a divorce eventually. *Perhaps I'm banking on the fact that you won't want to.*

She experienced a strange quiver. She wasn't sure if she

still completely understood Colin's motives, and that was troubling.

Her mother exchanged looks with Uncle Hugh and then addressed her. "Perhaps you might see Tod…in order to make amends."

Belinda's jaw dropped. "Make amends?"

"Yes, darling, in order to keep your options open. You will, after all, be a single woman again some day."

Belinda was flabbergasted. Here she'd been concerned about the possibility, however unlikely, of conceiving a child with Colin, and her mother was already thinking about her *next* husband.

Her mother had obviously not given up on the Dillinghams.

"You know I won't be around forever," Uncle Hugh joined in, "and Tod would make a good steward of the Wentworth estates."

"There are practically no Wentworth estates at the moment," Belinda retorted. "It's all in Granville hands."

It wasn't technically true. They still had one estate in Berkshire left, as well as a couple of rental buildings, but it hadn't been in the family that long. Still, at least they wouldn't be homeless, thank goodness, if Colin turned them out.

"This arrangement with Colin need be only a bump in the road," Uncle Hugh went on. "Surely once it's over, you'll wish to return to your rightful groom and pick up where you left off."

Belatedly, Belinda recognized just how much animosity her uncle harbored toward Colin, who'd divested him of the Wentworth patrimony. Uncle Hugh was ready to shoo her back in Tod's direction at a moment's notice.

Her mother was worse. She was almost suggesting that

Belinda befriend Tod and keep her options open, as it were, even before her marriage to Colin ended.

"Tod is no longer in the picture," Belinda responded flatly.

She reached forward and set her teacup down with more noise than necessary.

"Now, now, Belinda," her mother said in a soothing voice, "no need to get snappish. Your uncle means well."

"We're thinking of your best interests."

"Are you?" Belinda said as she stood up. "Then why is it up to me to save the family fortunes?"

She turned then and walked out the door.

She would head back to her London hotel, and then fly to New York to settle her affairs there.

Life had just taken a detour—one that led to Halstead Hall.

Seven

Belinda's eyes misted as Pia reached the front of the church.

Pia looked beautiful in her wedding gown, holding a tightly bunched bouquet of red roses. A delicate tiara graced her coiffure. It was a gift from Pia's groom, Hawk, for their wedding day.

In a nod to her groom's country, Pia had made a fashion-forward choice from a British designer. In a bow to tradition, however, the dress had lace elbow-length sleeves and a full skirt. The ensemble was light and ethereal, like Pia.

Belinda adjusted the skirt of Pia's dress and then took the bouquet from her friend's hands, all the while steadfastly refusing to make eye contact with Easterbridge, standing a few feet away, next to the groom.

The service was being held in the parish church near Silderly Park, the Duke of Hawkshire's estate in Oxford.

Belinda was Pia's lone attendant. Because Tamara was

several months' pregnant, she had bowed out of being part of the wedding party and had instead chosen to remain comfortably seated among the wedding guests.

To Belinda's discomfiture, however, Colin was acting as Hawk's best man. Belinda wondered if Pia's romantic nature was at work in the choice. After all, not so long ago, Pia had suggested that Easterbridge was drawn to Belinda like a moth to a flame.

Pia gave her a bright and tremulous smile before facing the minister.

Belinda was truly happy for her friend. But much as she hated to disillusion Pia, Belinda didn't think she and Easterbridge bore even a passing resemblance to Romeo and Juliet—though their families, she admitted to herself, might rival the Montagues and Capulets.

Belinda kept her eyes firmly on the Anglican minister as he began to speak. When the time came for the couple to recite their vows, though, her gaze drifted of its own volition to Easterbridge's.

"Wilt thou have this woman to be thy wedded wife…"

Colin's face remained cool and fixed, but his eyes were hot as they looked into hers.

"Wilt thou love her, comfort her, honour, and keep her in sickness and in health, and, forsaking all other, keep thee only unto her, so long as ye both shall live?"

Belinda felt herself heat, as if she could feel Colin's caress as well as see it. Every bone in her body seemed to melt under Colin's gaze.

The memory of their own wedding rose between them. It had been just the two of them, the officiant and standby witnesses called in by the chapel. Their service had been a lighthearted, can-you-believe-we're-actually-doing-this reverie. They'd both been looking forward to consummating their marriage.

"Wilt thou have this man to be thy wedded husband...?"

Once upon a time, Belinda thought, she'd answered yes to that question to the man standing a few feet from her and eating her up with his eyes.

"Wilt thou love him, comfort him, honour, and keep him in sickness and in health, and, forsaking all other, keep thee only unto him, so long as ye both shall live?"

Pia had chosen to modernize the traditional vows by omitting a reference to *obey* and instead using vows that mirrored the groom's.

Colin smiled ever so slightly.

Belinda raised her chin a fraction. Was he recalling that she similarly had chosen not to obey? It was a good thing, because the very next morning she'd chosen not even to *keep* him.

She recalled Colin's puzzlement and then thin-lipped control when she'd nearly bolted from their hotel room, horrified at her rash actions.

She had never imagined Easterbridge would agree to obtain a marriage license before she slept with him. She'd followed through rather than changed her mind because she'd been irresistibly drawn into his orbit by that point and Vegas was an uninhibited gambler's paradise.

It had been irresistibly seductive to be wanted so much. And now that Easterbridge was staking his claim on her again—moving heaven and earth to do so, in fact—she felt almost...cherished.

Belinda tingled down to the tips of her toes. Her gown was a modest peach chiffon confection, but under Colin's gaze, she felt as if she were wearing a revealing sexy ensemble, and enjoying its effect.

Colin looked as if he could lift her up right now and carry her down the aisle and directly to a bed—*his bed*.

At least, Belinda thought, she'd gotten desire if not love.

Easterbridge had given a vow to *love* her, but he couldn't have meant it—not after knowing each other so briefly.

She held back a sigh. It would be wonderful if a man could vow to love her and mean it. She'd never had the opportunity to test the proposition with Tod because their ceremony had been cut short. And with Easterbridge...

Because she felt unexpectedly teary, she drew herself up straighter.

Rats.

She would not give Easterbridge the satisfaction of seeing her get emotional. Though it was not unusual, of course, to cry at a wedding, she knew Colin would wonder if it was Pia's happiness or her own memories that had caused her tears.

Fortunately, she was able to make it through the rest of the ceremony without a hitch.

Later, at the wedding breakfast at Silderly Park, she found Pia and hugged her again.

Tamara walked up to them just as the quick embrace ended.

"I'd join the hug, too," Tamara quipped, looking down at her stomach, "if I didn't have a basketball in my way."

"I'm so very happy for you, Pia," Belinda said, blinking more rapidly than usual and then casting a glance at Tamara. "And for you, too, though you look ridiculously radiant as a pregnant lady."

"Only because my morning sickness has stopped." Tamara turned to Pia with a smile. "I suppose we'll need to address you as *Duchess* from now on."

"No, *ma'am* will do," Pia teased.

As a duchess, Pia outranked both Belinda and Tamara, who were marchioness and countess, respectively.

Belinda was sincerely glad that Pia and Tamara had found happiness with Colin's friends, the Duke of

Hawkshire and the Earl of Melton. Still, though to the outside world she might be a marchioness, Belinda knew that, unlike Pia and Tamara, her marriage wasn't built to last.

Sure, both Pia and Tamara had encountered roadblocks on the way to a happy marriage. Pia had had a fling with Hawkshire years before—when he'd represented himself as simple Mr. James Fielding—that had ended with her feeling discarded until their reunion years later gave him a second chance to earn, and this time, keep her love. Tamara, in contrast, had entered into a marriage of convenience with Melton that had turned into a love match. But Belinda doubted that a similar happy ending was in store for her and Easterbridge.

As if reading her mind, Pia leaned in conspiratorially. "What is happening with you and Easterbridge?"

"It's your wedding day," Belinda protested. "Let's not talk about other matters."

"I'm already pulling rank as a newly minted duchess," Pia teased.

Belinda knew Pia meant well, and since Tamara looked on with interest, she reluctantly gave in. "I suppose then that this is as good a time as any to tell you I'm no longer pursuing a way to dissolve my marriage to Easterbridge."

Pia clasped her hands together. "Oh, Belinda, that's wonderful news. You and Colin have decided to try to make it work."

Tamara looked doubtful. "I'm not so sure Belinda regards it as happy news, Pia. In fact, I'm guessing there's more to the situation than she's saying."

Pia widened her eyes. "Is that true?"

Belinda sighed. "I did warn you this wasn't a fitting discussion for a wedding day."

Pia touched her arm. "Oh, no."

"Let's just say Colin has plenty in common with Sawyer and Hawk in the complicated courtship department."

Pia looked surprised and Tamara resigned.

"He's blackmailing you?" Tamara hazarded a guess.

Belinda raised her eyebrows. "Why use an ugly word like *blackmail* when *proposition* will do?"

Tamara's eyes narrowed. "Just what is Easterbridge offering you?"

"Colin is now the proud owner of the Wentworth family town house in Mayfair, as well as the old estate in Berkshire."

Pia gasped, and Tamara's expression turned to one of sympathy.

Belinda resisted the urge to rub her temples. "Apparently, my uncle believed that the corporate entity to whom he was selling was a cloak for a wealthy foreigner who preferred anonymity. He didn't know it was Easterbridge until I broke the news to him recently."

"Uh-oh."

Belinda shot Pia a glance that said she agreed with the sentiment. "Of course, this change of ownership is all hush-hush. No one is supposed to know about it, and Uncle Hugh is continuing to reside at the town house in London."

"Well, don't worry," Pia said, "as far as I know, Mrs. Hollings hasn't gotten wind of this angle to the story."

Belinda frowned. "What do you mean by angle?"

Pia and Tamara exchanged looks, as if debating who was going to tell her.

"Out with it."

Pia pasted on a smile. "Mrs. Hollings published news in her gossip column this morning that you had moved into Halstead Hall and that you and Colin have decided to make a go of your marriage."

Belinda closed her eyes. "Oh, Pia, on your wedding day!"

"It's all right," Pia soothed. "My wedding will no doubt feature prominently in tomorrow's column. Mrs. Hollings' column is actually what prompted me to ask about you and Colin."

Belinda sighed. "I didn't want to trouble you with my news in the days before your wedding, and Tamara is pregnant and has other things on her mind."

The truth was also that she was still coming to terms with her new status quo with Colin.

Belinda had no idea how Mrs. Hollings got her information. The woman seemed to have sources everywhere. On the other hand, Belinda acknowledged that she herself had not gone to great trouble to conceal her steps, either. She had appeared on Colin's doorstep last week with weekend bag in hand and had let it slip at work that she'd been at Halstead Hall. For better or worse, she was going to be Colin's wife for the next two years, and word was bound to get out sooner or later.

She knew her marital status had been a source of speculation and interest at Lansing's, and elsewhere in New York and London. Everybody was aware of the debacle at St. Bart's last year—some had even been eyewitnesses.

She supposed that the silver lining to Mrs. Hollings' gossip column today was that her work colleagues would stop conjecturing about her marital status and see her as settled into married life.

Tamara fished a cell phone out of her small handbag. She scrolled down and then handed her phone to Belinda.

Belinda read the text with unease.

This columnist has it on good authority that a certain marquess and marchioness are nesting in Berkshire near H****. Could it be that a little birdie will hatch next spring?

Belinda mentally winced.

She handed the phone back to Tamara. "Isn't there something you can do to stop Mrs. Hollings? Doesn't she work for Sawyer's media outlets?"

Tamara shrugged as she put away the phone. "Mrs. Hollings is a renegade. Sawyer believes in the separation of the news and business sides of his companies. He won't interfere to kill an individual story."

Belinda grimaced at Mrs. Hollings' words. *Hatch a little birdie?* She hadn't even slept with Colin again—yet. She'd arrived back in England from New York just in time for Pia's wedding.

"What are you going to do?" Tamara asked.

Belinda lifted her shoulders. "What can I do? Nothing. No annulment, no divorce."

"So that's it? You plan to stay married...until death do you part?"

"Not quite," Belinda admitted, hedging. "I've talked Easterbridge into a sort of postnuptial agreement. The longer we stay married, the more Wentworth property I can walk away with in a divorce."

In fact, Easterbridge had had a short agreement drawn up by his solicitor while Belinda had gone back to New York. She'd had her lawyer review it, and the agreement had been signed just yesterday.

Pia looked deflated. "Still, perhaps Colin really does care for you, because what other incentive would he have for agreeing to such an arrangement?"

"Hardly," Belinda responded.

Tamara tilted her head. "And so, you're planning to stay the course in this marriage until you gain title to all the Wentworth property?"

"Exactly."

Belinda watched Pia and Tamara exchange another look.

"Just be careful," Tamara finally spoke. "Take it from me, this marriage of mutual convenience situation can be trickier than you think."

Belinda knew Tamara was remembering her own predicament with Sawyer, when her future husband had also made marriage a condition to the both of them getting what they wanted.

Belinda bit her bottom lip. "I've already learned my lesson, remember? I eloped with Easterbridge once. It's not the type of mistake that I intend to make again."

She knew she had to keep her guard up with Colin. She didn't have a crystal ball or good insight into his motivations.

Pia looked doubtful. "Well, this time you're already married, so the only thing that can happen is—"

Warningly, Tamara gave a quick shake of the head.

"—anything," Belinda acknowledged, finishing for her.

At the wedding reception, Colin barely took his eyes off of Belinda. He stood to one side of the ballroom and took a sip of his wine. He knew he had unmasked desire on his face. He was committing the unbelievably gauche sin of lusting after his own wife at a social event, but he didn't give a damn.

After Pia and Hawk's wedding ceremony, followed by a traditional wedding breakfast, everyone had repaired and refreshed in time for an elegant black-tie dinner-dance in Silderly Park's ballroom.

When Colin had first caught sight of Belinda tonight, she had stunned him with a body-hugging gown of crimson satin. She wore a large ruby-and-diamond pendant necklace and matching earrings. A delicate flower-motif tiara nested in her upswept hair.

He'd presented her with the jewels when she'd arrived at their hotel for the wedding. He'd texted her in advance to ask the color of her dress, and if she'd wondered why he bothered asking, she hadn't let on. He meant tonight to be a statement to everyone that Belinda was his marchioness. Not only were many entrants in *Debrett's Peerage* in attendance, but he thought he'd spotted a photographer for *Tatler,* the society glossy.

Across the room, Colin stared at the ruby pendant resting in the deep V of Belinda's cleavage. It twinkled and taunted him. If he thought he'd been tempted this morning during the wedding ceremony, he was certainly in purgatory now as a result of her crimson fire ensemble. It was all he could do not to sweep up Belinda and carry her away from the conversation that she was having with a Spanish countess.

Belinda had arrived from London only this morning and had parked her bags in their hotel suite with just enough time to get ready for the wedding. He'd missed her this past week. If anything, their recent skirmishes had increased his desire for her.

Colin handed his empty glass to a passing waiter and walked deliberately toward his wife.

At the last moment, Belinda turned her head and spotted him. She widened her eyes.

"Hello, darling," he said, leaning in to give her a quick peck on the cheek before she could move away.

The Spanish countess smiled at both of them.

"Colin, may I introduce you to—"

"We already have made each others' acquaintance," he interrupted smoothly. "Pleased to see you again, Countess."

"Likewise, my lord."

He cupped Belinda's elbow. "You would not mind if I lure my beautiful wife away for a dance…"

The countess smiled again and inclined her head. "Of course, not."

"Oh, but—"

Colin turned Belinda in the direction of the dance floor. "The next song is about to begin."

After a moment's resistance, Belinda let him guide her toward some other couples.

When they reached the dance floor, he turned her to face him.

She frowned up at him. "Neatly done."

It wasn't a compliment. Nonetheless, he smiled easily. "Thank you. I assume you know how to waltz?"

"Yes." She wrinkled her nose. "I was forced to take comportment lessons as a teenager."

His smile widened into a grin. "I can see the results. Your manners are exquisite, particularly toward me."

"Sarcasm is not appreciated," she grumbled.

He slipped his hand around her waist, and when she laid her hand in his, he pulled her closer.

She sucked in a startled breath. "Of course a romantic like Pia would want the waltz played at her wedding."

"Lucky me."

He'd been itching to touch her all evening, even if it was through the satiny barrier of her dress.

The music began, and they started gliding in circles around the dance floor, keeping time with the other couples.

Colin's eyes stayed on Belinda's as the world receded around them and they were swept away by the notes of "Waves of the Danube."

Her eyes were more amber than green. They reflected

her emotion in a way that she probably wouldn't be happy about but that was fascinating and useful for a gambler at heart like him.

Right now, her eyes were telling him that she was affected by their nearness although she was trying hard not to let it show.

He could feel her body heat under his hand at the small of her back. Her lips were slightly parted and carried a lustrous red shimmer that called to him.

The look of her lips just saved him from being entranced by the ruby practically tucked in her bodice. If it was gauche to gaze hungrily at one's wife, then staring at her cleavage was beyond the pale.

"If you keep regarding me that way, we may go up in flames," she said sharply.

"You're the one wearing red."

"Yes, it was clever of you to lend me jewels that are magnificent as well as a flashing fire alarm right over my cleavage."

He choked back a laugh. "Someone needs to put a warning sign on you."

"More like a stamp of ownership—"

He inclined his head and didn't deny it—so she had understood his intentions with his gift.

"—As well as a clever excuse for you to stare at my breasts."

He looked down just to annoy her. They still hadn't broken a step of the dance, and she kept a smile fixed firmly on her face.

"It is a stunning ruby," he murmured, "surrounded as it is by diamonds and the pillow of your creamy breasts. I was imagining the same when I chose the necklace and the tiara from among the jewelry in the family safe.

The earrings, however, I picked out myself this week at Garrard."

She shot him a look of liquid fire that nevertheless said she didn't know how to react. Should she be angry with him for his sexual banter, thank him for his gift or give in to the attraction that was undeniable between them?

The dance came to an end at that moment. He reluctantly loosened his hold on her, and stepped back.

"Walk with me in the garden."

She looked at him in surprise. "What? It's cold outside."

"Hawk has a greenhouse. It's where the head gardener works his magic for the estate grounds."

"I hardly think—"

"We're supposed to convince people tonight that we've decided to make a real go of our marriage."

It was a weak excuse. Still, she could not have missed the curious looks they'd received throughout the day.

She sighed.

"You know you want a breather. It's become a terrible crush in here." Particularly for them—a couple who was one of the interesting sideshows of the evening.

She contemplated him for a second, and then a look of resignation crossed her face. "Fine. I'll make a dignified exit with you."

They walked through the ballroom and out the French doors to a terrace warmed by heated lamps. From there, it was a short stroll to the greenhouse.

They discovered that Hawk's heated sanctuary had drawn other curious guests. They had come to admire some of the estate's more exotic plants and small blooms.

He and Belinda wandered along, stopping occasionally for her to appreciate a particular plant species—and for him to pretend to.

The greenhouse door opened and closed a couple of

times until Colin glanced around to discover that he and Belinda were alone except for another couple at the other end of the glass building. He could barely hear their voices.

"I believe Hawk's gardener has been experimenting to create hybrid roses," Belinda remarked.

She was looking down at a wood work table strewn with various gardening tools, plants and neatly marked glass jars.

He studied her profile. "I wouldn't be surprised. Max, my gardener, has done the same at Halstead Hall."

She cast him a look from under her lashes, as if wondering whether his comment was meant to be a reproach—his house, which was now her own as well, had the same cottage industry in place and she didn't seem to know it—or whether it was yet another meaning-laden invitation to make herself at home in his life.

The scent of roses and other blooms hung around them in the warm, humid air. Colin would never have thought that a greenhouse would be a sexually stimulating environment, but it was.

He let his fingertips trail up Belinda's arm in a light caress, and watched goose bumps appear. *Fascinating.*

She didn't look up at him, but there was a new stillness to her.

Testing, he stepped closer and cupped her upper arms from behind her. He bent and breathed in the soft air by her temple.

"What are you doing?" There was a catch in her voice.

"What does it seem as if I'm doing?" he responded, his voice laced with laughter and seduction. "I'm trying to determine your scent."

"There are other people here."

"Surely they won't mind if I try to distinguish my wife's scent from among those intermingled in the air."

"They'll misconstrue your actions."

"Is that my fault?" he murmured, teasing.

The greenhouse door opened and closed again, and this time, they were well and truly alone.

He stroked her arms. Belinda had the softest skin. He'd thought so before, but now, touching her, the tactile sensation brought the realization rushing back to him. Blood rushed to his head and other parts of his anatomy.

He let his lips skim the column of her neck.

"I don't think you'll be able to pick up my scent in a place as aromatic as this."

"Tiger lily," he announced, and then breathed in deep. "It's soap or body wash or some type of lotion."

She glanced back at him, her look astonished. "How did you guess?"

He crinkled his eyes as he held back a grin. "It's not a shy scent—"

"Oh."

"—and I noticed some tiger-lily products among your cosmetic products back at the hotel."

"Oh!" Her eyebrows drew together.

"I'm not nearly so omniscient about taste, however."

"Clearly."

"For that, there's only one way for me to find out."

Before she could react, he turned her toward him.

He settled his lips on hers and tasted her as if he had all the time in the world. He explored with his tongue, coaxing a reaction from her and inviting her to be a full participant with him.

After a moment, she relaxed in his arms, though she still didn't give him the uninhibited reaction he was looking for.

She tasted faintly of sweet wine and delicacy.

He worked hard to lower her defenses. His hands smoothed over her back, molding her to him.

She was a fantastic kisser. He'd learned that back in Vegas, and he got further glimmerings of her potential now.

He skimmed his hands above the back of her dress. He pressed and rubbed her muscles, soothing her.

Belinda made a low sound of pleasure.

Of course, he'd suggested the greenhouse in order to have a private moment, but he knew, even in his current aroused state, that he couldn't simply lower her to the floor here and make love to her.

Then again, he *could* lock the greenhouse door...

He undid the hook at the back of her dress and then lowered the zipper, relaxing her bodice.

Belinda sighed, and the cups of her gown fell away from her breasts.

Colin feasted on the sight.

Belinda's lips were parted and glistening, her eyes half-closed. The tips of her breasts were drawn tight, beckoning to him.

He bent and lowered his mouth to one rosy bud.

Belinda's knees buckled, nearly taking them both down to the floor.

Colin drew his brows together, concentrating on the task at hand—giving and receiving pleasure.

He breathed deeply, and Belinda moaned.

Suddenly, the greenhouse door opened and shut. A moment later, the air around them changed and cooled. Distantly, there was the sound of voices.

Belinda pulled away from him with a jerk and gathered her bodice to her chest.

He knew he should have locked that door when he'd had the chance.

She looked disheveled and reached to pull up her zipper. "We can't do this!"

"Reluctantly, I have to agree. We're no longer alone."

"Our postnup hasn't been signed," she countered.

"Is that what you're waiting for?"

"That's what *we're* waiting for," she corrected.

Clearly, she meant to hold him off on sex until the agreement was signed.

Colin breathed in deep and took a moment to bring himself back from acute arousal. Damn, it hurt.

No doubt about it. He'd have to raise hell to get their agreement finalized as soon as possible.

Belinda glanced from side to side and then shot him a repressive look. "I have to get out of here."

Colin smiled sardonically. He needed to get out of here, too. They had to leave before he got them to take up where they had unsatisfyingly left off—agreement or no agreement.

He raised her chin and touched the pad of his thumb to the corner of her mouth.

Her eyes widened.

"Your lipstick is smeared, and your color is high—"

She lowered her shoulders.

"—and sooner or later you're going to wind up in my bed."

She froze and then abruptly pulled away from him. "Yes, but for now, I need to freshen up and get presentable again."

She headed to the greenhouse door, and he followed her at a more leisurely pace.

He knew Belinda desired him—Granville or not.

His job was to make her *acknowledge* it. He felt as if he was on the verge of attaining a goal that he'd been pursuing ever since their night in Vegas.

Soon—very soon—Belinda would be his not only in name.

Eight

Belinda looked around her lavish bedroom at Halstead Hall. She had known luxury in the past, but this was at a whole other level.

The bedroom curtains were of silk damask, the walls were painted a celestial blue and the furniture was all carved wood antique. Her bed was large and canopied, the fireplace mantel was marble and a Victorian vanity table graced the far wall. The view out the windows was, of course, the best in the house. The vista was of the back lawn and wooded area.

This bedroom and its adjacent sitting room comprised the traditional quarters of the Marchioness of Easterbridge. The marquess' rooms were next door. Belinda had no doubt that Colin hoped to persuade her to go there at the first opportunity.

The fact that their postnuptial agreement had yet to be signed had bought her a reprieve. But Belinda had heard from her lawyer, and knew Colin was working diligently on getting the agreement finalized ever since Pia's wedding last week.

Belinda got goose bumps just thinking about it. She'd slept with Colin once, and it had been an earth-moving event for her.

She sucked in a deep breath. Her interlude with Colin in the greenhouse was still fresh in her mind. She remembered the feel of his mouth on her breast and of his hands on her skin. They'd been imprinted on her memory and came to her at night, unbidden.

She *couldn't* let him get under her skin so easily. She reminded herself of all his misdeeds—most of all, secretly buying up Wentworth properties.

She was just a tool to him. He was either toying with her or she was part of a grand plan that she wasn't totally privy to—or both.

Fortunately, she'd kept herself occupied enough to avoid dwelling on matters and to stay out of Colin's way.

In the past week, she'd flown to New York, tidied up her affairs there and asked for some time away from work until she was settled at Halstead Hall.

Her superiors at Lansing's had already broached the subject of transferring her to the London office on a permanent basis. Apparently, they were easily impressed by Colin's wealth and title and by the social and business connections implied by them. Everyone was intent on making nice and assumed moving her to London was what *she* wanted, too.

For now, she'd let her work colleagues think what they would, but she knew that she'd eventually have to clarify matters before she really was transferred to London.

She wanted to disrupt her life as little as possible, as vain a hope as that might be, even though she'd chosen to remain married to Colin. She knew Colin spent a good deal of time in New York seeing to his business interests. Let him accommodate *her* in his life, as well.

After glancing at her watch, Belinda left her bedroom and headed downstairs for a late lunch. Colin was still in London, roughly an hour's commute away, attending to pressing work matters.

She turned a corner in the hallway and steeled herself when she realized Colin's mother was coming her way.

The dowager marchioness had moved out of the house when her husband had died, ceding Halstead Hall to Colin as a principal residence and staying primarily at an address in London's tony Knightsbridge neighborhood. Belinda had gleaned that much from Colin and the staff.

Regardless, however, the marchioness was visiting here today, and by the looks of it, she was just as surprised and nonplussed about encountering the newest member of the family as Belinda was about meeting her.

Colin's mother must have just arrived, Belinda thought. According to the staff, the dowager was used to availing herself of Halstead Hall during travels and in lieu of a hotel when visiting the neighborhood.

The dowager marchioness inclined her head at the same time as Belinda nodded in greeting.

The older woman didn't crack a real smile. "Settling in?"

"Yes, thank you." Belinda was sure the news wasn't welcome.

"You'll want to speak to the chef about the menu for next week's dinner party," the other woman said, coming to a stop. "And the housekeeper, Mrs. Brown, is looking for direction as to how you wish your work space organized. I believe a number of social invitations are awaiting your response."

Having stopped, too, Belinda pasted a smile on her

face. "I am looking forward to meeting with Mrs. Brown tomorrow."

"Excellent."

"I'll speak with the chef."

"You are unused to how we run things at Halstead Hall."

It was hard to argue with the facts. "Yes, I would say so."

"An important realization."

"One of many, I hope."

With that, the dowager marchioness sailed on, and the two of them passed each other like two ships with canons manned but holding most of their fire—at least for now.

Belinda sighed. She wondered how many such skirmishes she was destined to have.

As if fate laughed, she descended the stairs and ran into Sophie.

The other woman looked uneasy. "Good afternoon."

"Good afternoon."

"I just arrived. I came to Halstead for the weekend to pick up some of my things, and I plan to leave tomorrow."

Colin's sister stopped as if out of breath—and as if belatedly realizing that her words could be construed to mean that she was gathering up her belongings and clearing out now that Belinda was living in the house.

What could she say in response, Belinda thought, that could not also be misconstrued? *Take your time? Let me know if I may be of help?*

She sensed that Sophie didn't bear her as much hostility as her mother but, rather, was finding the whole situation awkward and strange.

Belinda could hardly blame her. She and Colin's sister were contemporaries, but they'd never had any real interaction. Public events such as Royal Ascot and Wimbledon were big enough to lend themselves to selective socializing by Granvilles and Wentworths alike.

Belinda opened her mouth and voiced the first passably sensible thought that occurred to her. "I've yet to discover an art room in the house."

"There isn't one," Sophie said.

"Didn't you ever have one?" Belinda asked curiously. "With your profession…"

"I did most of my work outside the house and then took many of my things with me when I moved into a London flat. Mother didn't approve of graphic des—"

Sophie cut herself off.

Belinda was glad *she* wasn't the only person or thing that Colin's mother frowned upon. "Perhaps I'll create a room, then. I'm sure the youngest Granville cousins would appreciate it, and the staff must have children and grandchildren who would."

Seemingly despite herself, Sophie showed a spark of interest.

Belinda felt surprisingly heartened at the positive sign. She and Colin's sister were both in artistic professions, and she wouldn't be surprised if Colin's sister had an appreciation for nineteenth- and twentieth-century artwork. Maybe the next two years wouldn't be as bad as she'd feared.

"Sophie?"

The dowager marchioness's voice sounded from above them, and Sophie shot Belinda a rueful look before heading up the stairs.

Belinda continued on to the dining room.

Perhaps, she thought, all was not lost. Or at least, she'd survived another day…

There was something incongruous about a marquess doing his own grocery shopping. Belinda watched Colin eye a display of imported tapenade and other spreads.

She'd been at Halstead Hall a couple of days when Colin had returned. When he'd realized she was making a trip to the supermarket, he'd decided to come along—to her chagrin.

She pulled a crunchy French loaf from a bin and deposited the bread in her shopping cart. She rolled her cart a few feet, and stopped next to Colin.

Her brow furrowed. "How often do you run out to buy your own milk?"

Colin looked amused. "Now and then."

She searched his face.

"More so now," he teased, "that there's a marchioness who insists on selecting her own brand of jam."

"Except I didn't know I was a marchioness for all of the past three years."

"If William and Catherine can be caught buying their own produce at the market," he joked with a reference to the British royals, "then I suppose a marquess can, too."

"We are in Waitrose, however," she countered. "I refuse to be too impressed."

She knew just as well as he did that the upscale supermarket chain, run by a workers' cooperative, was popular in well-heeled social circles.

Colin smiled. "I'll just have to keep trying, then."

Her eyes skated away from his as she was conscious of the air between them changing.

She continued on with her cart, and Colin turned to follow.

She scanned the shelves, glad for the distraction. While it was safe to think of Colin as all aristocratic hauteur, she had to admit that he'd pleasantly surprised her with today's outing.

They continued on through Waitrose, stopping to chat with the occasional local who recognized Colin as the local marquess. At each conversation, Colin introduced her as his wife. There were no looks of surprise, presumably because everyone in this corner of Berkshire was well aware of the recent notoriety of the Marquess and Marchioness of Easterbridge.

Belinda was relieved not to have to offer any delicate explanations about how she'd become Colin's wife—particularly since there'd been no recent wedding celebration. Or at least, she corrected with an inward wince, there had been no wedding in which she'd been the bride and Colin had been the *groom*.

Still, even though their grocery shopping went smoothly, she was glad when they reached the checkout.

They stood in line like everyone else. Colin paid by credit card and then declined assistance to their car by one of the baggers.

"No need," Colin said to the teenager. "I'll have no problem handling these bags myself."

When they exited the supermarket, she followed Colin to their vehicle, where he loaded their purchases. Then she waited while he began to wheel their empty cart back toward Waitrose.

He'd only gone a few feet, however, when a petite older woman, well-dressed and carrying a Chanel purse, stopped him.

"Young man, would you mind assisting me inside with a return purchase? If you could simply bring your cart over here." She gestured to the back of her car.

Belinda realized that the woman had mistaken Colin for a Waitrose employee or manager. Perhaps the Chanel lady thought that Colin was reporting for his shift and had decided to tidy up the parking lot by taking an empty shopping cart inside with him.

Belinda opened her mouth. "Oh, but—"

She cut herself off as she caught Colin's eye and his slight shake of the head.

She gave an almost imperceptible lift of her shoulders.

Within minutes, Colin had loaded the woman's medium-size espresso maker into the cart.

Belinda watched as the older woman followed Colin toward the store entrance.

They'd only gone a few yards when a real Waitrose employee spotted them, froze and then hurried over.

On a mischievous impulse, Belinda started forward herself.

"Oh, dear," she announced in a voice meant to carry.

Colin and the Chanel lady turned back toward her.

"So sorry," she said, looking at Colin apologetically, "but I forgot to tip you."

Colin cast her a droll look, and she returned it with an impish smile before lifting her handbag from her shoulder.

A male Waitrose employee stopped before them. "May I be of assistance, my lord?"

Belinda caught the sudden arrested expression on the other woman's face. The *my lord* was, of course, a giveaway. Only certain members of the aristocracy were addressed in that fashion.

"Oh, my." The Chanel lady looked abashed as she glanced from Colin to Belinda and back. "I had no idea. I'm new to the area—"

"May I introduce you to the Marquess of Easterbridge?" Belinda deadpanned.

The older woman's eyes widened as she continued to regard Colin.

"I'm happy to be of assistance, madam."

"I—oh, goodness."

"It's all right," he said smoothly. "I usually go by the code name Colin."

The Waitrose employee looked baffled.

Belinda nearly giggled.

Colin bent toward her and murmured, "If you can go by the alias Belinda Wentworth, why can't I be Chuck the grocer?"

"First of all, your name is not Chuck," she whispered back. "And secondly, you're to the manor born."

"So are you."

She cast him a sidelong look. "It's different. I didn't grow up as the heir, nor am I the current holder of a marquessate."

Colin looked ready to say more, but she turned back to the other woman.

Belinda leaned forward conspiratorially. "He's a good-looking clerk but not nearly as impressive as a lord, don't you think?"

If possible, the other woman looked even more flustered. She glanced up at Colin. "My husband and I would be delighted to have you over for tea, my lord. To thank you for your assistance, of course."

Colin scanned the cart beside him. "I suppose espresso is out of the question?"

The woman tittered. "The coffeemaker can be replaced."

Belinda smiled. "We're most appreciative of the invitation."

Colin sighed. "May I introduce my wife…?"

He proceeded to do so.

The store employee looked undecided as to what to do.

Colin gave him a small nod. "If you would be so kind as to assist this lovely lady inside with her purchase?"

"Yes, of course, my lord."

"Excellent."

Belinda waited beside Colin as the older woman and

the store employee moved off and then turned back with him to their car.

Colin spoke first. "Thank you for accepting an invitation to tea."

"You're welcome," Belinda responded tongue-in-cheek. "Except she didn't get your address."

"I'm sure a few inquiries will yield my coordinates at Halstead Hall."

"How often have you done that?"

"What?"

She waved a hand back toward where they had come. "You know, *that.*"

"It happens from time to time."

"It was a rather nice thing to do," she allowed. "Rather classy to not immediately correct her misimpression but just offer your assistance."

She tried hard not to feel charmed, but still felt herself slipping.

"She called me *young man,*" Colin remarked as he walked beside her. "I suppose it's all a matter of perspective, but still it's worth a few points in my book."

"It's no more than you deserve," she scolded with mock humor, "for taking a trip to the supermarket dressed so unassumingly that you might be mistaken for anyone."

"Would you prefer I wear a pin declaring me a lord? Or better yet, a Granville?"

"Please."

Colin gave an uneven grin. "I suppose it would be easier than facing the awful possibility that not all Granvilles are died-in-the-wool villains."

They reached their car, and Colin pulled open the passenger door for her.

Belinda glanced up at him but found her gaze skittering

away again. They were getting into uncomfortably deep waters.

"Now, about that tip that you owe a certain good-looking store employee…"

There was laughter in Colin's voice, and it brushed tantalizingly across her skin as he let her pull the car door closed.

From the doorway, Colin watched Belinda exchange smiles with his cousin's nine-year-old daughter.

Daphne was standing before an easel, and Belinda was encouraging the girl, as well as pointing out a few ways to deepen the painting.

The empty playroom next door to what traditionally functioned as the nursery, on the third floor of the house, had been turned into a painting studio and an arts-and-crafts room. Canvas covered the wood floor, and the curtain-free windows offered an unobstructed path for the morning sunlight.

A half-dozen children moved about. Everyone wore paint-smeared smocks over casual clothes and sneakers or clogs. Some retrieved art supplies and others stood intently before easels. One child was the ten-year-old daughter of his stable manager, and another was the housekeeper's grandson. There was also Daphne's seven-year-old younger sister, Emily.

Belinda had suggested setting up an art playroom once she'd heard there were definitely children in his extended family and among the family of the staff. The art classes had been a big hit. At least those Granvilles below the age of twelve had taken to Belinda naturally. And Sophie had admitted to spending some time in the art room working with the kids alongside Belinda.

Colin thrust his hands into his pockets. Belinda's guard

was down, probably because she hadn't yet noticed his appearance in the open doorway.

He took the opportunity to study her.

Similar to the kids, she was dressed down in jeans and a pullover lavender top. The jeans showed off a pert rear end, though her smock obscured the rest of what Colin knew to be a delicious figure. Her hair was caught back loosely, but tendrils escaped to caress and frame her face.

Colin felt a tightening in his gut.

Daphne gave an impish grin, and Belinda laughed down at her. It was clear Belinda was in her element—spattered with paint and laughing. And she was relaxed, naturally, all because she thought he wasn't there.

In the next moment, however, she glanced up and caught his eye. She froze, and he gave her a mocking salute with a lift of his lips.

For him, every look and glance was overlaid with the memory from Vegas of kissing her luscious pink lips, smoothing his hand down a satin thigh and tracing a path along the tender skin of her abdomen.

Belinda quickly looked down to answer another of Daphne's questions.

When Daphne finally moved off, Colin sauntered in.

Belinda glanced at him warily.

"Who knew that what was missing was an art room?"

She gave him a tart look. "Well, it does already possess a double-height library, two wine cellars and a private theater."

He let his eyes crinkle. "Welcome to the ancestral pile."

"Is there any element I've overlooked?"

"No worries. You've added the missing element. An art room."

"You're the one who has a Renoir hanging in the master suite."

"Perhaps I was hoping to tempt you."

Belinda reddened. "Thank you, but I'm perfectly content with reproductions in books."

He laughed softly. "Any time you change your mind…"

"I won't."

"The agreement is awaiting your review and signature."

They both knew which contract he was referring to. It was the postnuptial accord that she had set up as the final barrier between them.

Belinda turned away. "Yes, I know. I'll get to it as soon as I have the chance."

"Don't wait too long."

He laced the words with promise. He watched Belinda's profile stain with heat again before she walked over to help another child.

Colin watched her go.

He'd stayed away in London and New York on business for a week, he'd taken cold showers and pressed his attorney to act fast. Let Belinda feel some of his urgency.

He knew he had to keep up the heat. He *would* seduce his wife back into his bed.

And then his plan to make Belinda acknowledge she wanted a Granville—that their night in Vegas was no fluke—would be achieved.

Frankly, his sanity was starting to depend on it.

Nine

When Colin had suggested they attend a performance at Covent Garden, Belinda had been unable to resist agreeing. She knew *Aïda* was playing. She'd always thought the opera was unbearably beautiful.

One of the things she'd always loved about the southern corner of Berkshire where Downlands and Halstead Hall were located was that it was just a short trip to London, making a night in town more than possible.

She was happy and excited when Colin bought tickets for good seats, which she knew were expensive and often hard to come by. She wanted to think he'd thought of her when doing so, but she was also enough of a realist to remember Uncle Hugh's words: since Colin had suffered a blow to his ego when she'd nearly walked down the aisle with another man, of course he'd be eager to line up public engagements for the two of them.

She dressed with care in a one-shouldered midnight-blue cocktail dress and croc-embossed peep-toe pumps. She had caught back her hair in a loose knot. She knew Colin would be in a suit and tie.

In fact, her heart palpitated excitedly as she came down the main staircase at Halstead Hall, all the while aware of Colin, handsome and distinguished, looking up at her from the landing.

Their postnup had just been finalized—she'd reviewed and signed it—so there was nothing barring Colin from her bed anymore. She also knew this was the twenty-first century and a marquess couldn't just order her around. Still, she knew that she was morally obligated to stand by her agreement.

She tried to focus on the fact that she had signed a contract. She wouldn't let herself think about standing face-to-face with Colin in his bedroom, his hot eyes on her while his hands skimmed over her sensitized skin, making her desperate with the desire for him to undress her.

She wouldn't think about the pleasure to be found in his arms.

No, she wouldn't.

Because they dined at home, they went directly to London's Royal Opera House in Covent Garden for the performance. Colin drove them in his Aston Martin, eschewing the services of Halstead Hall's resident driver.

Inside the opera house, the crowd was already milling. Colin introduced her to a couple of acquaintances who greeted him, and Belinda thought she did a credible job of smiling and being an appropriate consort.

When she and Colin eventually ended their conversations and made their way up to their seats in a front box, she had trouble relaxing. She almost wished Pia and Tamara were there for support. At least their husbands were friends of Colin's with whom she was familiar and comfortable.

When she and Colin took their seats with a close view of the stage, Belinda caught her breath. No need for opera glasses, she thought whimsically. The view was spectacular.

She perused her program until, minutes later, the lights blinked and dimmed, signaling the beginning of the performance.

She was just sliding into the start of the opera when Colin clasped her hand, folding it gently into his. She couldn't help focusing on the contact.

His hand was bigger, tougher and rougher than hers. It was an apt metaphor for their relationship, she thought. Yet, his clasp was surprisingly gentle, and his lightest touch had an electric effect on her.

She felt tossed by a storm of emotion mimicking the drama onstage. There were two shows here tonight—the one in which the singers participated, and Colin's private one for her benefit.

He traced over her hand with his thumb—an airy and rhythmic movement that might be mistaken for a soothing motion but that caused a quickening tempo of tension inside her.

She stole a glance at him from the corner of her eye. He faced forward and his face gave nothing away—except he continued his light touch on her hand.

She admitted that Colin had quite charmed her lately. Logically, she wished it were otherwise, but she was finding him hard to resist.

Belinda parted her lips on a sigh as she focused on the stage again.

The military commander, Radames, was caught between his love for Aïda, a captured princess, and loyalty to his Pharaoh—whose daughter, Amneris, had unrequited love for her father's commanding officer.

Belinda felt her heart clench as the opera built to its tragic climax. She almost couldn't bear to watch the final scene, where Radames and Aïda were destined to die together.

She swallowed hard against the lump in her throat and blinked rapidly. Belatedly, she became aware of Colin squeezing her hand, his thumb smoothing over the pulse at her inner wrist.

The audience burst into applause as the final scene faded to its close. Belinda bit her lip and distractedly accepted Colin's offer of a tissue. She felt silly—she'd known how Verdi's opera ended. But still, she cried.

She told herself that the image of star-crossed lovers was iconic. Radames and Aïda were the Romeo and Juliet of another era. Neither couple bore any resemblance to her and Colin—*not in the least.*

"Did you enjoy the performance?" Colin asked, his voice deep and low.

"I loved it," she croaked.

He chuckled then, and she gave a weak laugh—because her tears clashed with her statement.

"Let's get home."

Belinda felt a rush of emotion at Colin's words. It was the first time he'd used the word *home* with her to refer to Halstead Hall, but of course she knew what he meant without thought. Had she already started to think of Halstead Hall as home?

They rode back in companionable silence, making desultory conversation.

"I thought I'd make you happy with tickets to *Aïda,*" Colin joked at one point, "but it would seem you prefer to cry when you go to the opera."

"You weren't unaffected by the performance, either," she parried. "You wouldn't be an opera fan otherwise."

He cast her a sidelong look, taking his eyes off the road for a moment. A smile played at his lips. "I was enjoying watching you as much as the opera singers on stage."

She heated. "You were not watching me!"

"How do you know?"

She bit her lip, because of course she had been found out. The only way she could know for sure that he hadn't been watching *her* was by being aware of *him*.

"I know," she insisted. "You were too busy playing with my hand."

Colin laughed, low and deep, and then faced the road again.

Belinda glanced out the window. They were speeding toward Halstead Hall and already the air between them had become more intimate.

When they arrived at the house, everything was still and dark. Colin had told the butler not to await their return from London. Some of the staff, of course, had the day off.

Belinda hesitated in the hall, unsure of what to do.

"Nightcap?" Colin asked, offering a solution to her problem.

"All right." She nodded, willing to put off the climb up the stairs to their adjoining suites.

She followed him into the library, where she disposed of her evening bag and coat while Colin busied himself at the side bar.

When Colin returned, she gratefully accepted the glass of clear liquid on ice from him.

"Cheers," he toasted, raising his glass. "To new beginnings."

She took a sip at the same time as he did, and her eyes widened. "Water?"

"Of course."

He took her glass from her and set both glasses down on his nearby desk.

This was not what she'd envisioned when he'd suggested a nightcap. She'd pictured imbibing something strong—to fortify her.

Colin trailed one finger up her arm to her shoulder. "It's a good thing neither of us has had a real drink."

"Why?" she asked, stumbling over the word. "So we don't do anything rash and regret it again?"

He gave a small smile. "No, so we won't have any excuses when we do."

Belinda's heart beat a staccato rhythm in her chest. "We have to stop this."

"Do we?" he joked, and then looked around. "Last time I checked, we were married. We even live here."

"The marquess ravishing his wife in the library? It sounds like a bad round of Clue."

"If I weren't so aroused right now, I might suggest we play."

"Isn't that what we're doing? Playing?" she parried. "This is a game."

"Then why am I so deathly serious?"

"Because you play to win."

"Exactly. Kiss me."

"Rather direct," she tried. "I would have thought you'd have more subtle lures in your repertoire."

"I do, but I've waited three years."

"Perhaps the first time was a fluke."

"Does this feel like a fluke?" He took her hand and placed it on his chest. "Touch me, Belinda."

Belinda's head buzzed. She felt the strong and steady beat of his heart beneath her palm. The contact with him was intoxicating, just like at the opera.

"We may have been born and bred to be enemies," he said, "but in this, we're one."

"It's just passion…"

"Enough to build on."

Colin bent his head slowly, tilting it first in one direction and then in another, as if deciding how he wanted to kiss her.

Belinda felt as if the moment drew out forever.

When he finally settled his lips on hers, it was with soft but insistent pressure, and Belinda unconsciously parted her lips.

He tasted faintly minty and all male, a flavor that only fueled and deepened her desire. His hands settled on her shoulders, where they molded and relaxed her.

She'd closed the door on their past. She'd tried not to dwell on how hotly passionate their night in Vegas had been. Now, however, she recalled vividly how he'd kissed every inch of her.

Her nipples became pronounced, her hips heavy with desire.

Colin moved his hands down her back.

"I don't know where the zipper is," he murmured between kisses.

"That's the point," she said against his mouth.

"I don't want to ruin your lovely dress. It fits you like a glove, and with any luck, there'll be other evenings when you can wear it to bring me to my knees."

She fought against the feelings that his words evoked. "You are not literally on your knees."

He pulled back to gaze into her eyes. "Would you like me to be?"

She trembled because she remembered the previous time that Colin had called her bluff. They had walked into a wedding chapel.

He trailed a finger lazily down from her collarbone to her cleavage, just skirting the tip of one breast.

"If I were on my knees," he said in a deep voice, "I think my lips would reach right here."

He touched the sensitive skin of her midriff.

She found herself holding her breath.

"On the other hand, if you bent forward," he continued, "my mouth would close over here."

His thumb skimmed over her nipple, and Belinda gasped and her eyes went wide.

"Would you bend over for me?"

"I—it's a theoretical question," she responded thickly.

"But it doesn't have to be."

He settled his lips on hers again, and Belinda's response was muted.

This time, rather than holding still, he folded her into his arms, and she slid her hands around his shoulders.

Colin found the zipper hidden in the side seam of her dress. He lowered it slowly, and cool air hit her skin.

Colin trailed his lips across her jaw to the delicate shell of her ear and then down toward her throat.

Images, words and scents from their night in Vegas came back to her. They'd been joking and teasing...until suddenly they weren't. Instead, they'd lain back on the bed, entangled in passion.

It had been the best sex of her life. Colin had been tender, prepared and patient—that is, he had been until a powerful climax had shaken him and sent her over the top with its aftershocks.

And now he was doing it again.

The dress slipped away from her.

Colin took a step back so that he perched on the corner of his desk. "Come here. Please."

If he'd been arrogant or impatient, she'd have had a

chance at resisting him. Instead, she took two steps forward and fit in the space created by his legs.

He leaned forward, and his lips nuzzled her cleavage.

Belinda's eyes drifted closed.

He licked first the tip of one breast and then of the other, stoking a fever of emotion inside her.

She moaned, and her fingers spread through his hair.

Colin settled his mouth on one breast, and Belinda arched up to him.

She felt deliciously alive, her body humming with desire. She rubbed against Colin's erection, the evidence of his burgeoning passion.

Colin groaned and turned his attention to her other breast.

It was all too much and yet not enough, Belinda thought hazily. It was consuming and liberating.

Their clothes fell away from them, one by one, until only Colin's trousers remained as a barrier between them.

With her gown and panties pooled at her feet, he lifted her, not breaking their kiss.

Her high-heeled pumps hit the library floor with a thud, one after the other.

Colin strode with her across the room and stopped next to the sofa. She slid down his body, feeling every hard plane and muscle on the way, her breasts grazing the sparse hair on his chest, until her feet touched the ground.

A low fire burned in the hearth nearby, casting shadows on the Oriental rug before it.

She looked up at Colin. "I thought we'd be safe in a room without a bed."

He grazed her temple with his lips. "There are ways around it. And we've already tried a bed."

"The Renoir hangs in your bedroom. Isn't that the key to your seduction?"

He gave a choked laugh. "Call it arrogance, call it flying without a net, but maybe I thought I would be enough."

Colin skimmed his hands over her thighs and then up her back.

Together, they lowered to the sofa, and he leaned over her.

His eyes glittering down at her, he cupped her intimately. He parted her folds and dipped inside her. She clenched around him instinctively.

She felt the caress of his thumb at her most intimately guarded place. Her eyelids lowered, and she bit down hard on her lip. Waves of sensation lapped her.

"You drive me crazy when you do that."

"Oh." Then she realized she wasn't sure what he meant. "Oh?"

"I keep thinking of sucking on that pouty lower lip of yours."

Unthinkingly, she bit her lip again.

"I want you." Already shirtless, he stood up and disposed of his trousers, and then sheathed himself with protection that he retrieved from a pocket.

The flames from the fire cast their flickering shadows on him, showing him in all his bronze glory.

He was magnificent—primed and male and wanting her. *Right now.*

Liquid fire coursed through Belinda.

Colin lowered himself to her, settling himself between her legs.

"I'm sure this sofa is an antique," she protested.

"Then it's been witness to plenty."

Without another word, he glided inside her, causing them both to sigh.

It had been so long—three years—that Belinda found

herself trembling. A tremor went through Colin, too. She could feel it.

He began a rhythm that she soon took up in counterpoint, her fingers finding traction on the dips and plateaus of the muscles of his back.

They both moaned.

"That's right," Colin urged.

"Yes." The blistering word was all she could manage.

The sofa groaned and creaked with their increasingly urgent movements.

They were so hot for each other that it was a wonder their coupling wasn't over in minutes.

She was impressed by Colin's control in order to give and receive pleasure. He was making it good for her, just as he had in Vegas.

Waves lapped her with increasing strength until she felt herself undulating with climax.

She cried out and Colin held her, soothing her.

Minutes later, he built his rhythm again, until he suddenly stilled and gave a hoarse groan.

Belinda followed him over the edge again on a throaty cry.

Afterward, they lay together, spent and breathless.

If there was any doubt, Belinda thought, about their first time being a fluke, it had been put to rest.

Ten

"Congratulations, Melton."

Colin glanced around him after offering the words. He and Sawyer, along with Hawk, were sitting in the library of Sawyer's London abode, a luxury flat in Mayfair. Tamara, Sawyer's wife, had come home from the hospital yesterday, after giving birth to Viscount Averil. She, Pia and Belinda had gone to the nursery with the baby.

"Thank you," Sawyer said in acknowledgment of his words. "In lieu of cigars, I'll suggest a round of scotch."

"It is a rather stupendous occasion," Hawk remarked.

"Rather," Colin commented. "The newly arrived viscount is in fine form, though he came a little early."

Belinda had received a call that Tamara had given birth, a few days after the trip to Covent Garden. Colin had driven them to London at one of the earliest opportunities.

Still, his brief time at Halstead Hall with Belinda had been spectacular, Colin thought with an inner grin. Three years had not dimmed his memory of their wedding night in Las Vegas, and the night of the opera had been a fitting sequel.

He felt a bone-deep sense of rightness—like turning up an ace at the end of a card game. Certainly, it wasn't a feeling that he'd gotten with any other woman.

Now all that remained was to get Belinda to acknowledge aloud that he, a dreaded Granville, had the same effect on her. It was all that remained, but it was a tall order.

"The baby's arrival caught both me and Tamara by surprise," Sawyer said, breaking into Colin's thoughts. "Though since he weighed seven pounds, perhaps it was a good thing that Tamara didn't go on for even another week."

"Thanks to Tamara's dual citizenship," Colin remarked, "the little viscount will also be an *American* heir to the earldom."

Sawyer rose and headed to the bar. "I'm sure one of my ancestors is rolling in his grave right now. Probably one of those who was among George III's cronies."

"No doubt."

"Tamara rather liked the idea of—"

"—snubbing one of your starchy ancestors?" Hawk finished.

Sawyer turned back and smiled. "I'm just relieved we were within walking distance of a hospital when Tamara went into labor. And now with the baby, we're heading in a new direction."

Hawk addressed Colin. "Speaking of new directions, you and Belinda appear to be on more amicable footing these days, Easterbridge."

Colin cast him a droll but forbearing look. "You mean she doesn't seem to be on the verge of doing me in?"

Sawyer looked up, pausing in the act of pouring scotch into a double old-fashioned. "One can't help but note the subdued fireworks."

"Meaning there still are some?"

Hawk tilted his head. "I'm surprised I haven't enjoyed more barbed comments between you and Belinda up to now."

"Yes, rather unsporting of me not to provide more entertainment," Colin commented drily.

"We do have empathy for you, Easterbridge," Sawyer put in, walking back with three glasses in his hands, "because we were in your shoes ourselves not too long ago."

Colin knew that neither Hawk nor Sawyer had had a smooth path to the altar with their wives. And yet, both were happily married now.

"Still, it is interesting to watch how the mighty have fallen," Hawk added with a grin, accepting a glass.

Colin quirked a brow. "What makes you think I've fallen—or even kneeled?"

Hawk and Sawyer exchanged looks before Hawk looked back at Colin with a sly smile. "Then I'll look forward to witnessing it happen when it does."

Colin felt his cell phone vibrate, fished it out of his pocket, and glanced down for a moment at the screen.

"Congratulate me, gentlemen," he announced, accepting his own glass from Sawyer. "You're looking at the new owner of the Wentworth's Elmer Street property."

Hawk's eyebrows shot up. "You've bought another Wentworth property in London?"

"Only a minor one."

"And let me guess," Sawyer said, "you did not reveal yourself in this real-estate deal, either."

"Only to those who know the exact constituency of the firm Halbridge Properties," Colin returned blandly.

Hawk shook his head in resignation. "You got Halbridge from combining Halstead and Easterbridge, I suppose. Clever."

Colin said nothing.

"You're in deep waters," Hawk commented finally.

Sawyer nodded his head in agreement. "Be careful, Easterbridge. Much as I admire your prowess in business, you're in uncharted territory here."

"I'm used to high stakes," Colin replied blandly, raising his glass in anticipation of a toast to the new arrival. "Bring it on."

Belinda looked down at the newborn Viscount Averil sleeping in his crib and her heart constricted. Tamara and Sawyer had named the baby Elliott, but by virtue of his father's name and position, he carried a courtesy title and thus was styled Elliott Langsford, Viscount Averil.

Belinda cast a glance around the nursery, done in shades of soft gray and white, before looking down at the baby again. She, Pia and a proud but tired Tamara hovered over the crib.

Two days ago, Belinda reflected, she'd again had the best sex of her life. It had been glorious, liberating and disconcerting at the same time. If she was in the same room as Colin, she wanted to throw herself at him. And from the looks of him, Colin stood ready to catch her at a moment's notice.

Yet, she knew it was temporary. Their agreement was for two years. There would never be a sleeping baby with downy skin making soft breathing noises, his torso rising and falling with every rapid beat of his heart. She and Colin had used protection to ensure it.

Belinda swallowed. She told herself that her emotion stemmed from the fact that she wouldn't be a mother at least until after she and Colin parted ways. Of course, she didn't want to become pregnant. *Of course*—it wasn't part of her understanding with Colin.

"Should we sit down?" Pia whispered, looking from Tamara to Belinda and back.

Belinda shot Tamara a look of concern.

Tamara's smile was weary but transcendent. "Only if I have a donut pillow to sit on."

Pia giggled and then all three of them moved toward the doorway and into the adjacent playroom.

Tamara sat in a rocking chair while Pia removed a stuffed giraffe from its position and sat on a toy chest.

Belinda made herself comfortable in a perch on a child-size chair.

She looked around the brightly colored playroom, a contrast to the nursery next door. "You know," she quipped, "I think I need to get back to playing with a primary palette and get away from all this impressionist stuff."

Tamara and Pia laughed.

Tamara gestured to the bookshelves set against a far wall. "Your watercolors await you. We're stocked for kids of all ages."

Pia tilted her head to the side. "Speaking of playing, you and Colin are acting positively cozy. Did I imagine it, or did he give you a warm kiss soon after you walked in the door together?"

Belinda flushed.

Pia was a true romantic, but Belinda didn't want to give her friend false hope. The truth was that she and Colin had become lovers. *But* they didn't have a permanent relationship, despite being married.

Tamara sat up straighter. "Something tells me that Belinda is looking at Colin more kindly these days."

Pia clapped her hands. "Oh, good. I always thought you and Colin should—"

"It's not what you think," Belinda said.

Tamara arched a brow. "Worse?"

How had her friend guessed? She was susceptible to Colin, more so than she had wanted to admit.

Belinda hesitated and then confessed, "Diary, I slept with him."

Pia gasped.

Tamara laughed. "We've all been there and now I have a baby to prove it."

Exactly, Belinda thought. In contrast, there'd be no baby for her—at least with Colin. She shifted in her seat.

"Just be careful," Tamara said. "I'm afraid that Colin is cut from the same cloth as his two counterparts sitting downstairs—Pia's husband and, much as I love him, mine. In other words, he should come with a warning label."

She hardly needed the warning, Belinda thought, when the sensible part of her wholly agreed.

"The path of true love never runs smooth," Pia offered.

Belinda knew Pia wouldn't be quelled in her romantic notions, but neither would the continuing complicated history of the Granvilles and the Wentworths.

Two days after visiting Sawyer and Tamara, Belinda prepared to attend a dinner-dance with Colin on an estate near Halstead Hall in honor of a new exhibition of eighteenth-century Chinese art. The guests were to be treated to an advance private viewing.

Belinda wondered if Colin had wanted to accept the invitation to please her, because he knew art was her passion as well as her career.

She scanned the contents of her closet. She moved aside one hanger after another. Though Colin had announced she had her own funds as the Marchioness of Easterbridge, she had decided to wear a gown that she already owned.

She didn't really have time to shop. What's more, she already owned a small but formal wardrobe because her career required her to attend the occasional black-tie affair. She'd paid for her designer wardrobe by carefully budgeting her funds and shopping the sales.

After debating a few minutes, she chose a floor-length beige tulle and beaded dress that cleverly skimmed her curves. Its color matched and blended with her skin tone.

Later that night, Colin's reaction didn't disappoint.

When she walked into the parlor where he was awaiting her, his face took on an appreciative expression.

Belinda felt her pulse pick up—and not only because of the look on Colin's face. If she thought she'd ever get used to him in a tuxedo, she was being proved mightily wrong.

He had an old-world elegance. His hair gleamed glossy dark in the light, and he looked impossibly broad and masculine in his suit.

The chauffeur appeared in the doorway. "I will await you outside at the car, my lord."

Colin's eyes flickered away from her for an instant. "Very well, Thomas."

Belinda composed herself. The flower-motif tiara that Colin had previously given her was nestled in her upswept hair.

"You look…" Colin's voice trailed away, as if he'd been robbed of words. "Ethereal."

She felt the words like a caress. "Thank you."

"I have something for you."

She watched as he reached for a velvet case on a nearby table and then approached her.

He opened the case for her inspection, and her breath caught.

"Yet again, it appears we're on the same wavelength," he commented, his tone deep.

The velvet case contained a dazzling diamond choker. The styling marked it as vintage, probably from the Victorian or Edwardian era.

"It came into the family by way of my great-great-grandmother." There was a smile in Colin's voice. "She wasn't a Granville by birth."

Belinda glanced up at him. "It's lovely." She swallowed. "I'll need a moment to put it on."

"No need," he said, the words falling easily from his lips. "I'll help you."

She searched his gaze, and what she saw there sent her heart into deep beats.

Colin set the box down and removed the diamond sparkler. It gleamed with white fire in the light.

She held herself still as he leaned close.

The cool diamonds slid against her skin, and a moment later, Colin's warm fingers touched her as he worked to fasten the jewelry at her neck.

Belinda felt her nipples tighten in reaction, and warmth pooled within her.

When his job was done, Colin paused, his lips hovering inches away from hers.

Her breath hitched in response.

They remained that way for only a fraction of a minute, but it seemed like forever.

"I'm looking forward to this evening," Colin said huskily.

Yes. No, no. What was wrong with her?

He had her so confused and sexually aware that she couldn't think straight.

Colin straightened and gave her a lopsided smile. "I believe I'll let you deal with the matching earrings yourself."

The spell was broken. Belinda took a step back.

In the next moment, Colin reached for another velvet box, she turned toward a nearby oval mirror and the housekeeper simultaneously walked in to announce that rain was threatening and umbrellas were advisable.

Soon after, Belinda and Colin departed for the party. The short drive was uneventful, and since this wasn't her first social engagement with him, she soon found herself relaxing and enjoying the party when they arrived.

Two of Colin's married cousins were present—parents of children that she'd entertained in the art room. After some awkward chitchat with her, they and their spouses appeared to lower their defenses—if only because she'd so effectively entertained the junior members of the family.

A little while later, she was turning away from a conversation with a British viscount and his wife when she spotted a familiar figure and froze.

Tod.

She was aghast.

She had no idea that he would be here tonight. She glanced over at Colin and realized that he had noted Tod's presence, too.

Belinda stifled the impulse to bolt. She supposed it was inevitable that she and Colin would run into Tod at some point. London was not that big of a town. Still, did it have to be right now?

Tod approached her. "Lady Wentworth—or is it more proper to address you as Lady Granville?"

Within a moment, Colin had walked over to them and

gave Tod a sharp nod of acknowledgment. "In either case, she is the Marchioness of Easterbridge."

Belinda looked at Colin. Must he refer to the elephant in the room so bluntly? All three of them knew she remained Colin's wife. Tod had asked a fair question given that she'd retained her maiden name and a number of people knew it.

Still, annoyed as she was with Colin, she couldn't help comparing the two men as they stood side by side. Tod seemed somehow diminished in Colin's presence. He was not quite as broad, but there was also a subtle distinction in bearing. Colin exuded power.

Of course, the physical differences were only part of the story. Tod had given in to familial pressure by heading to the altar with her. In contrast, Colin had eloped with her in Las Vegas, driven by passion and acting in careless defiance of what his family might have thought.

Tod turned toward her. "Would you like to dance?"

"Her next dance is taken." Colin spoke before she could.

Belinda felt her annoyance kick up a notch. Before she could say something, however, Colin and Tod faced off.

Tod raised his eyebrows. "The dance after that, then."

"It is taken, as well."

"Belinda can speak for herself."

"There's no need when I've already answered you."

Belinda looked from Colin's set expression—he looked practically menacing—to Tod's clenched jaw. They seemed as if they were moments away from coming to blows. What's more, they were attracting curious looks from nearby guests.

"First you lock her into marriage," Tod muttered, "and now you're shuttering her away from the world?"

"In fact, Dillingham, you will notice if you look around you that Belinda is attending a social event." Colin's tone was icy.

"So it's me that you object to?"

"And as for marriage," Colin went on flatly, ignoring the question, "Belinda and I eloped because we couldn't keep our hands off each other."

Belinda gasped.

Colin's words were a thinly disguised insult. The implication, of course, was that she and Tod *had* been able to keep their hands off each other.

It didn't help that there was truth behind Colin's words.

Belinda could see a muscle flex in Tod's jaw, and Colin's hand had clenched at his side.

She quickly stepped between the two men.

"This is outrageous," she announced. "Stop this minute, both of you."

Because she'd had enough, she turned on her heel and stalked off.

As Belinda made her way through the crowd, trying not to draw attention to her hot face, she fumed about the imbecility of men.

To think that she'd befriended some of the extended Granville clan this evening. She'd even started believing that Colin might be more than an overbearing, conniving Granville.

Of course, Belinda thought, the only thing that people would remember now was Tod and Colin's tense standoff. The exchange had stopped short of being a full-blown scene, but she'd seen the looks on the faces of some nearby guests.

She'd agreed to remain married to Colin, but he didn't have a license to embarrass her—them—on his path to vanquish the Wentworths.

Belinda managed to avoid Colin—and Tod—for the rest of the party by making conversation with one fellow guest after another. As was customary at these formal functions, she and Colin, as husband and wife, were not seated next to each other at dinner. And neither, thank the fates, was she seated near Tod.

When it was time to depart, she and Colin had reunited for only the most desultory conversation. They rode home in silence in their chauffeured car.

And when they arrived back at Halstead Hall, she sprinted lightly up the stairs to her suite while Colin stopped to speak with the butler.

Finally closeted in her rooms, Belinda felt her nerves ease for the first time in hours. She sat down at her vanity and removed her jewelry.

She stared at her face in the mirror. The woman who looked back at her was composed, belying the roil of emotions inside her. Her makeup was still in place, her hazel eyes luminous but wide—as if she was still trying to process tonight's drama.

At any moment, she expected to hear Colin's tread in the hallway as he made his way to his own suite, but she heard nothing.

Belinda pressed her lips together. The longer that Colin remained downstairs, the more her anger grew.

How dare he?

After debating for several minutes what to do, she rose and turned and made her way out of her suite and downstairs.

When she reached the lower level, she could hear movement from the library, but otherwise the house was quiet.

She walked into the library, and Colin looked up.

He had a decanter in one hand and a glass in the other. His tuxedo tie hung loose around his neck. Despite looking uncharacteristically careworn, however, he was still devastatingly attractive.

"Drink?" he offered.

She shook her head.

"As you wish," he said, returning to the task of pouring himself one.

His abruptness was startling. It was unlike Colin to be anything but effortlessly well-mannered, even when he was vanquishing an opponent.

"You were an absolute boar to Tod."

"Was I?" Colin returned. "I suppose you mean the animal and not that I bored him to death, however appealing the thought might be."

Belinda pressed her lips together.

Colin turned back toward her and took a sip of his drink. "Were you also afraid I'd gore him?"

"Only with your rancid wit."

"Ouch." Colin shook his head. "And what about the way you wound me, my dear wife?"

Belinda blinked.

"I'm a servant who awaits your next word and hangs on your every glance."

"That's the most ridiculous thing I've ever heard."

Colin quirked a brow. "Is it?"

He set down his glass and come toward her.

Belinda forced herself to stand her ground. "Our agreement does not give you license to be rude to Tod."

"Doesn't it?" Colin asked. "And what about the fact that you almost wed him while you were still married to me?"

"I didn't know that we were still married."

"But now you do."

He was talking circles around her, and she tried to formulate a response that would expose his illogic. Just because she knew now what she didn't know then, she wasn't at fault, was she?

Colin appeared to anticipate her argument as he came to a stop before her. "It happened without your knowing, but now we must all be cognizant of the fact that it did happen, and also that you remain married to me."

Colin was jealous. And it rendered him surprisingly vulnerable.

The realization flashed through Belinda's mind unbidden and unwanted. To stay mad at Colin, she didn't need a surprising insight into his perspective.

He touched her upper arm and a shot of sensation went through her. She knew Colin had noticed the reaction in her, too.

"It's always there between us, isn't it?" he murmured.

It was hard to argue with the truth.

He gave a self-derisive chuckle. "Definitely inconvenient at times."

"Like right now."

He shook his head. "I need to kiss you."

Colin claimed her lips before she could react.

Her moan remained stuck in her throat. Instead, she found herself wrapping herself around him even as his arms bound her to him.

They kissed frantically, kindred souls finding each other and trying to meld. Sexual union was only part of it.

Colin divested her of her gown and she kicked off her shoes.

"I wanted to wring Dillingham's pretty little neck when he wanted to dance with my nearly naked wife."

"I know." And she did—now. Oh, she still had the lingering remnants of anger, but she was more understanding.

They frantically worked at removing Colin's tie and then he shrugged out of his jacket and shirt.

She moved her fingertips over the smooth planes of his chest and then down to the hair above his groin.

He undid his belt and shed his trousers and shoes.

They were both nearly without clothes now.

He was fully aroused, his erection pushing against his briefs.

She caressed him through the fabric, letting her hand wander and explore.

"Yes, touch me," he said harshly.

She slid the briefs off of him and then kneeled and slowly caressed him with her lips.

"Belinda, sweet—"

She savored her effect on him until Colin pulled her up and tugged off her panties. They lowered to the sofa.

Belinda felt Colin's delicious weight press her back against the pillows. She wrapped her legs around him.

She thought dimly that Colin's library was fast becoming their favorite place. They really couldn't be bothered with a trek to bed most of the time.

Colin kissed along her jaw and down the side of her neck. His hand stroked up and down her thigh and then cupped her breast.

Their breathing deepened and mingled as Belinda's world shrank to the two of them and their need for each other.

Colin stopped only to reach for protection and then gathered her to him.

"You know," he teased, his voice rough with passion, "before you, I never considered the library to be a sexy place."

She batted her lashes. "Do you want me to play the role of the sexy librarian?"

He gave a bark of laughter. "Why not? You've already been my Las Vegas seductress."

"Your lucky charm and arm candy at the gaming tables?"

"Come here."

Colin claimed her in a blaze of passion that matched her own. And Belinda's last thought was that if she couldn't resist him now, she could never resist him.

She shut off her mind before she could follow that thought to its logical conclusion...

Eleven

As Colin rode his polo horse across the field, holding his mallet at the ready, Belinda fanned herself with her event program.

April was the beginning of polo season, and the weather was mild.

But the sight of Colin exerting himself, his legs encased in form-fitting riding breeches as he rode to and fro to help his team best their opponents, was having an odd effect on Belinda's body temperature.

They were on polo grounds near Halstead Hall for an event to raise money for a local children's hospital. Even though the sporting event was for a good cause, the players on the field played ferociously.

Competitiveness was part of Colin's nature, Belinda realized. Moreover, he was born and bred to win.

A week had passed since Belinda's path had unexpectedly crossed with Tod's and had set her and Colin into an emotionally and sexually charged confrontation.

The power balance between them had been altered. Colin's reaction that night a week ago had been so stark—almost pained—that it had pierced her heart. He was under her spell as much as she was under his. They were two bodies circling around each other in an intimate dance.

Since then, she was cognizant of the fact that he was a Granville, that they had a postnup and that he held Wentworth property in the palm of his hand. But she was also aware of her power—and of the fact that the relationship really came down to the two of them.

They had, in the past week, been unable to keep their hands off each other. She had lost track of where and when they had been intimate. Certainly they had been at night in his bedroom, which she had essentially moved into, but also in the library, in the sitting room and—she flushed at the recollection—even in the stables after they had gone horseback riding.

Colin was filling her mind as well as possessing her body. She was losing sight of the reason she was staying married to him—to get the Wentworth property back.

Her cell phone buzzed, and Belinda retrieved it from her handbag to realize that she had missed a call from Uncle Hugh because she had had her ringer turned off. She quickly listened to the phone message and its summons to Downlands.

She frowned. Uncle Hugh didn't sound in ill health, but he hadn't given a precise reason for his call, either. She wondered what was going on.

She sighed, pushing aside an uneasy feeling. There was no way around it. She would have to go see him and find out what the issue was. Fortunately, it was a short trip from Halstead Hall to Downlands.

She looked up and saw Colin walking off the polo field toward her. The skin at the open collar of his shirt glistened with perspiration, and there were damp patches on his clothes. She knew he would smell all male, and her body began to hum in response.

He stopped, leaned down and brushed his lips across hers.

When he straightened, he smiled. "We won."

"Did you? I didn't notice."

His smile widened. "We'll have to work on your appreciation for the sport of kings."

"Why?" she asked innocently, looking at him through her lashes. "Would you rather I didn't focus on you instead?"

"Well, in that case, I can hardly argue."

He bent down and kissed her again.

Belinda's mind swam as she was quickly surrounded by his scent, his touch and his taste. He was quickly becoming addictive.

"We're in public," she managed when he drew back.

"To the victor go the spoils, as they say." He looked wicked. "Can I interest you in a trip to the stables?"

She tried and failed to look prim. "We've already been there."

"Go with what works."

She felt herself flush. "I really can't at the moment. I received a rather cryptic message from Uncle Hugh, and I need to check on him at Downlands and make sure nothing is seriously amiss."

"I'll wait for you at Halstead Hall, then."

There was promise in his words.

When Belinda arrived at Downlands, she found Uncle Hugh pacing in the library.

She'd had so many happy moments in this house while growing up. Downlands was smaller and less impressive than Halstead Hall, but it boasted light and airy rooms, courtesy of an Elizabethan frame that had been added, and lovely gardens. It was hard to believe the place had been sold.

"What is the matter?" Belinda asked.

Uncle Hugh turned toward her, looking agitated.

When her uncle didn't immediately answer, she truly began to worry. "Unless it's life or death, I'm sure—"

"Your husband bought and sold the Elmer Street property."

"What?" Belinda tried and failed to wrap her mind around what her uncle had just said. "Bought and sold? When and how?"

She hadn't even known the Elmer Street property had been on the market. It was a four-story residential building in Covent Garden that was rented out. The rentals had probably made it a more difficult property to sell.

Uncle Hugh rubbed his hands together. "I sold it to a company called Halbridge Properties. I just discovered the firm is another front for your husband, and he, the bounder, has promptly turned around and tried to sell the Elmer Street address to someone else."

Belinda felt her heart plummet. "You sold another Wentworth property?"

She felt betrayed—by all sides. Hadn't she put herself on the line trying to get back ownership to property that her uncle had already unwittingly sold to Colin? How could her uncle do this to her?

She spoke the last thought aloud. "How could you sell another property?"

"Belinda, please. You have no idea how dire our finances are."

"Apparently not."

Uncle Hugh continued to look distressed.

"And to be taken by Colin, again."

At this, her uncle flushed.

In Uncle Hugh's defense, Belinda had to admit that her uncle was probably not the only one to have been roundly bested by Colin. She'd seen firsthand what a good gambler Colin was. And his skill extended to real estate. He was London's most famous landowning marquess.

He was also the man who'd made tender and passionate love to her.

All along, however, he'd been intent on buying and selling yet another Wentworth parcel.

She felt betrayed and, worse, sullied.

"How is your relationship with Easterbridge?" her uncle asked suddenly. "You had no idea about Halbridge Properties and its recent purchase?"

This time, it was her turn to feel uncomfortable. She thought about Colin making sweet love to her. She'd thought they were growing closer, she'd thought that…

Never mind. It was clear that all the while, Colin was keeping her in the dark about his machinations with respect to the Wentworths.

Uncle Hugh tilted his head, his expression betraying a mixture of desperation and cunning. "There's always room for negotiation between a husband and wife. You worked your magic on Easterbridge before, perhaps…"

Uncle Hugh let the sentence trail off, but Belinda nevertheless understood his meaning. He had hopes that she could seduce back the Elmer Street property from Colin, too.

If she needed any further evidence, her uncle's implication highlighted how much her marriage to Colin was viewed simply as a means to an end by her family. *She* was merely a tool.

Belinda wanted to say that the way she was feeling right

now, the Berkshires would turn into the Sahara before she'd sleep with Colin again.

She swung toward the door. Yet again, she thought grimly, she was destined for a confrontation with Colin.

Colin turned toward the door of his home office at Halstead Hall.

When he saw Belinda, a swell of pleasure coursed through him. She was still dressed in the attire she'd had on at the polo field earlier—knee-high black boots and a tweed dress cinched by a thin belt. He couldn't wait to undress her.

He'd just had time to shower and put on some clean clothes, but he'd be happy to strip down again for her if it meant getting her into bed—or for that matter, even without a bed.

In fact, he was tempted to lock his office door right now...

He cut the distance between them.

"How could you?" Belinda demanded.

In the process of bending to kiss her, Colin pulled back and arched a brow. "How could I what?"

"You bought, and then promptly turned around and sold, the Elmer Street property without anyone being the wiser."

He stilled. She'd caught him off guard. He'd meant to tell her and explain why his actions made sense, but now he had to improvise.

"How did you find out?" he asked without inflection.

"Uncle Hugh informed me."

"Fine chap, Uncle Hugh."

Belinda continued to frown at him. "A business associate of his discovered the truth. He investigated

Halbridge Properties and told Uncle Hugh who the true owner was."

"Of course," Colin said drily. "Why am I not surprised Uncle Hugh has been keeping his ear to the ground? Or should I say, more accurately, has friends doing it for him?"

"Yes, well, at least he has the Wentworth family interests at heart!"

"Does he?" Colin countered. "He sold the property in the first place. And in this case, I agree with him. The Elmer Street property is not in good shape. It needed to be sold, and the proceeds need to be used to upgrade the other Wentworth properties."

If possible, Belinda looked more irate. "So you admit that you intended to sell as soon as you bought the property?"

He said nothing, and she read her own meaning into his silence.

"Does everything with you come down to a decision based on numbers?" she asked. "What about emotion and sentiment? I can't believe you are the same person who eloped with me in Vegas."

Colin tightened his jaw. "What makes you think marrying you wasn't my biggest gamble?"

"So that's what it was to you?" she countered. "Another calculation of risk and potential payoff?"

He thought he was doing her—and the Wentworths—a good turn by bringing some sanity to their financial chaos. Of course, he'd anticipated that Belinda's initial reaction might be negative, so he'd been looking for the right moment to explain. But now she'd discovered matters for herself in the worst way possible, and she showed no signs of being able to see his side.

"I said it was a gamble, not that emotion didn't enter

into it," he responded. "The Elmer Street property is of sentimental value to you? You never even lived there."

She tilted up her chin. "It's been in the Wentworth family for two generations."

"And that line of thinking demonstrates precisely why the Wentworths found themselves in a financial fix."

"I'm a Wentworth." She placed her hands on her hips. "We had an agreement. You promised not to sell Wentworth property."

"I promised to sign over to you the Wentworth property that I owned. The Elmer Street property is one that I subsequently bought."

Belinda fumed. "No wonder Uncle Hugh didn't suspect you were the buyer. He thought you were bound by our postnuptial agreement."

"I am bound by it, and I haven't broken it."

"You still violated the spirit, if not the letter, of our agreement. We agreed to stay married partly to keep Wentworth property together."

"And it will. The proceeds from the sale of the Elmer Street address will be well-spent on upgrades to the other Wentworth properties."

"What guarantee do I have that you'll actually use the money to renovate the other properties? After all, you sold the Elmer Street house without informing me."

Colin felt his annoyance spike. All he was trying to do was help her loony relatives out of their financial quicksand. "I didn't promise a day-to-day update on the management of the properties."

"There is nothing to say, then, is there?" she countered.

Belinda turned on her heel and walked toward the door.

Belinda watched Uncle Hugh frown.

"There are rumors and gossip in the press that you left

Colin," Uncle Hugh said, grasping the arms of his chair, "and they depict you in an unflattering light, I'm afraid."

Her mother, sitting gingerly to Uncle Hugh's right, nodded in agreement.

Frankly, Belinda didn't give a fig about rumors. She was more miserable than she could ever remember being, including when she'd bolted from a certain Vegas hotel room.

They were in the parlor of Uncle Hugh's Mayfair town house—or rather, her husband's Mayfair house. It was all such a tangle.

After leaving Halstead Hall yesterday, she had spent the night at Tamara and Sawyer's empty London flat. Tamara hadn't hesitated to lend her the apartment as a place to stay, particularly since she, Sawyer and the baby were back at the family seat in Gloucestershire.

Her friend had been a bit curious about the reasons behind Belinda's unexpected phone call, but the emotions had been too raw for Belinda to talk about them.

She was fortunate, Belinda thought, that no one had been witness to her sleepless, teary night. She'd tossed and turned to no avail, and the tears had continued to seep from under her lids.

By dawn, she had been unable to escape the truth.

She loved Colin's intelligence, his humor, and, yes, his sexual skill. They had common interests, but more importantly, they complemented each other in personality. He made her feel more alive.

She had fallen in love with Colin.

It was why his betrayal was like a dagger to the heart.

But obviously, she was nothing more than a conquest to him. If he cared for her, he wouldn't have been so cavalier about his disposal of the Elmer Street property.

Uncle Hugh drummed his fingers on the arms of his chair.

He had come down to London from Downlands earlier in the day. Upon learning that Belinda was in town, too, he had suggested that she take tea with him and her mother.

Uncle Hugh glowered. "I'm sure the stories in the press were planted by the Granvilles. Well, they might have gained the initial upper hand in the media, but we'll win the war."

Belinda felt her heart squeeze. Had Colin retaliated in the press, making sure he fired the first salvo in a divorce battle?

Uncle Hugh rubbed his hands together. "We'll hire the best lawyers to contest Colin's sale. We'll claim he violated your postnuptial agreement. We'll request that you be granted all of the original Wentworth property in a divorce. When the property is back under my stewardship, I'll see to it that the Granvilles aren't allowed to touch it again."

"No."

The word caught her by surprise almost as much as it did her uncle and her mother.

Everyone stopped.

"No?" Uncle Hugh asked, his brow furrowing. "What do you mean, no?"

Belinda took a deep breath. "I mean I'll never give up control of the Wentworth estates."

Uncle Hugh relaxed. "Well, of course not, dear girl. Isn't that what we're trying to arrange, with any luck, and the help of a few good solicitors?"

Belinda suddenly saw things with a clarity that had hitherto eluded her.

Belinda knew in her heart that her uncle would simply start selling or mortgaging the properties to the hilt if he had control. Uncle Hugh was not competent to manage the Wentworth estates.

In a way, Belinda realized, Colin had done her and the Wentworths an immense favor. If Uncle Hugh hadn't unwittingly found an eager buyer in Colin, he may have stripped the properties to the point of default and foreclosure. And then the Wentworths would certainly have fallen out of favor with the upper crust. They would have stopped receiving party invitations and gotten the cold shoulder in certain quarters.

Her family had been keen for her to marry Tod, and she'd assumed they'd simply wanted her to make a good match. She hadn't been aware of how desperate they had been for her to save the family fortunes.

There was a big difference, she thought, between making it known that you were expected to marry up, and being sacrificed to save the family from financial ruin—again and again.

She loved her family, but they were human and flawed—very flawed.

What was it that Colin had said? She had a choice between being a stick-in-the-mud or a free agent.

Her uncle continued to look uncomprehending. "Of course, you'll have a property manager in me, or Tod when you marry him."

"No, Uncle Hugh," she said firmly. "Tod is out of the picture—for good. What's more, if and when I divorce Colin and have control of the Wentworth property again, we'll do things my way."

What a novel thought—her way.

Her mother looked quizzical. "Belinda, this is absurd."

"No, it's not," she responded and then stood to leave. "I think it's the best idea I've had in a long time. In fact, I'm rather looking forward to becoming a real-estate mogul."

Her husband had taught her a lot. And one of those things was that she had more power than she thought she had.

She had just asserted her power with her family. Now she had to decide what to do with respect to Colin.

She'd been unfair to him, she realized. He should have told her about the Elmer Street property, but with new insight, she understood why he had acted as he had with respect to the disposal of the building.

The only question was, how would she mend fences with him, and would he want her back after she had seemed to side with Uncle Hugh?

Twelve

"Mother, what have you done?"

"Never fear, dear. It's all about the media these days."

"Believe it or not," he said patiently, "I'm one of those relics who still believes in a reality apart from public perception."

"Nonsense. What an antiquated idea."

The irony, of course, Colin thought, was that *he* had brought the Granvilles into a new millennium, shoring up the family wealth through shrewd real-estate holdings.

They were sitting at lunch in a room with French doors that offered a panoramic view of the gardens of Halstead Hall. At one time, the room had functioned as the music room, but these days it served as the family's informal dining room.

He'd been informed by a member of the staff shortly before lunch that his mother had arrived and would be joining him for the meal. As usual, his mother had presented herself impeccably groomed, pearls in place.

He, meanwhile, felt uncharacteristically scraggly and under the weather. He hadn't shaved that morning, and though he wore his usual work-at-home attire of trousers and open-collar shirt, he felt unkempt.

He knew the cause of his mood, however. She had left two days ago.

His mother took a sip of her tea. "You know, you really could take a cue from your friend Melton. He's a media person, isn't he?"

Colin wondered sardonically if his mother included following Sawyer as an example in the marriage department. After all, Tamara, the earl's wife, was a maverick American by upbringing, though her father was a British viscount. On top of it all, she remained one of Belinda's closest friends.

"Melton will be hurt to discover that you didn't use one of his media outlets as your mouthpiece for a public statement," Colin drawled. "I will assure him, however, not to take the matter personally."

The dowager marchioness waved a hand dismissively. "I still begrudge that horrid columnist of his, Mrs. Hollings. How dare she perpetuate the story of your appearance at the Wentworth-Dillingham nuptials?"

"How nice of you to retaliate by *not* feeding her salacious gossip about Belinda."

"It's the least I could do," his mother sniffed. "And I don't understand what you're upset about. What did I say that wasn't true? Belinda left you after you bought some burdensome property and thus gave much-needed financial assistance to the Wentworths."

"I'm not sure Belinda would characterize matters in quite that way."

The marchioness raised her eyebrows. "Precisely my point."

In the two days since Belinda had left Halstead Hall, he'd had time to reflect and, frankly, brood. It had been hell and he'd been unable to work.

He'd started to think that Belinda had a point. He'd been so fixated on the bottom line that he'd somehow failed to appreciate how much Belinda cared about other things. Of course, family, history and sentiment were important to her. She was, after all, a lover of impressionist art, the epitome of nineteenth-century romance.

His mother sat up straighter. "We need to move quickly and gain the upper hand so that the press and public opinion are on our side. I'm only thinking of your reputation."

"My reputation doesn't need saving."

He needed saving. He needed Belinda to save his cerebral and mercenary gambler's soul.

Because he loved her.

The realization hit like a sledgehammer. He was flummoxed, right before exploding joy and worry hit.

It was a hell of a moment to have an epiphany, considering his mother was in the room. But there was no other explanation for the way he'd been feeling since Belinda had departed.

His mother looked at him consideringly. "Colin, you could have your pick of brides."

"Yes, and how could I forget that the story you planted in the press also listed the names of one or two women."

His mother's eyes gleamed. "Suitable ones. As I said, you could have your pick."

"But I want just one," he replied. "I can't believe you'd turn your back on Belinda so easily. The rest of the family has warmed to her."

"She's still a Wentworth."

"It's past time to bury the hatchet. The hostilities have lasted longer than the War of the Roses."

"Of course, the hostilities are over," his mother replied, frowning. "You have won. The Wentworths are in your debt."

"Have I won?" he asked softly.

His mother closed her eyes.

"Accustom yourself to the idea, Mother. Belinda is the Marchioness of Easterbridge, and if she'll have me, she'll remain so."

He knew with a sudden clear insight that, without Belinda, his seeming victory over the Wentworths would be hollow.

As Belinda opened the apartment door, her mouth dropped. "How did you find me?"

Colin's mouth lifted sardonically. "A little birdie told me."

"Sawyer," she guessed.

Colin inclined his head. "It is his flat, after all."

"I detest the way you blue bloods band together."

"And right now," he guessed, "you especially detest me."

She let her silence speak for itself. Of course, she was furious and hurt. Why shouldn't she be? She'd been falling for him while he'd been toying with her.

How could she castigate Uncle Hugh for his bad judgments, she thought, when she'd made worse decisions?

And yet, she found herself drinking in the sight of Colin. His hair was mussed, when it ordinarily looked smooth, and his jaw was shadowed, when he was normally groomed.

"May I come in?" he asked, his manner steady.

"Do I have a choice?"

"Sawyer has graciously lent me his apartment, too, while I'm in London."

"How kind of him." She lifted her chin. "One wonders at the need for it, considering just how many properties you have acquired lately."

"The Mayfair town house is rented out."

"Oh, yes, how can I forget? Your act of noblesse oblige. Uncle Hugh sends his regards."

Colin bit off a helpless laugh. "I suppose I deserve that."

"Surely your mother and sister would offer you a sofa to sleep on in London."

"Perhaps Sawyer thought my home was here with you."

Belinda felt suddenly flush with emotion.

"With so many properties at your disposal?" she forced herself to scoff.

Colin looked at her steadily. "As a matter of fact, those properties are the reason I'm here."

She tensed. "I thought you would have let your attorney do the talking."

He grimaced. "Do we have to have this discussion on the doorstep?"

Reluctantly, she moved out of the way.

He stepped inside and removed his overcoat. It was an overcast day, typical of London but not rainy—yet. Under his coat, he wore a white open-collar shirt over dark trousers.

Belinda was glad she was presentable herself, though she'd had to use cucumber patches for her puffy eyes this morning. She had, however, showered and dressed. She'd donned a blue belted shirtdress, tights and flats shortly before Colin's arrival.

After Colin folded his coat and placed it on a nearby chair, she turned and walked farther into the flat, leaving him to follow her.

She stopped in the parlor and turned back to face him.

Despite appearing a bit careworn, he was still imposing—tall, broad and ruthless. And yet she remembered his achingly soft caresses and his whispered words of promise.

Like a bad angel, she thought with a twist of the heart.

"The Elmer Street property is not being sold," he announced.

She blinked.

It had not been the announcement that she'd expected from him. She had thought he was here to negotiate with her about their future.

"I thought it was a done deal," she finally said.

"The sale was in contract, but the parties had yet to sign."

"Oh." She paused. "What made you change your mind?"

He searched her eyes. "I decided it would be better to sell the property to you—"

She frowned.

"—for one pound sterling. Have you got it in your purse?"

Her heart skittered. "Is this some attempt to modify our postnuptial agreement?"

"Yes, for forever."

Her eyes went wide.

Colin stepped toward her, and she caught her breath.

He acted like his usual commanding self, but his face told a different story. It spoke of stark need and naked emotion.

"What are the terms?" she asked with a catch in her voice.

"Name them." He searched her face. "In fact, my plan is to sign over all the Wentworth property to you today for a nominal amount…and for accepting me back, if you'll have me."

Belinda felt emotion clog her throat. Still, she managed to say, "Of course, you would never be caught without a plan."

Colin lifted his mouth in an uneven grin. "A gambler always has a strategy, and I believe this is one of my better ones."

"Oh?" she asked, matching his tone. "Then far be it for me to stand in the way of its execution."

"Excellent." He went down on bended knee and took hold of her hand. "Belinda, would you do me the great honor of remaining my wife?"

She blinked back tears. "Even better."

"I love you passionately."

"Best. Definitely the best plan you've ever had." She smoothed away an errant tear. "I love you, too, so I suppose there's nothing for it but to remain married to you."

It was hard to say who moved first, but in the next moment, they were in each others' arms and kissing passionately.

It was a long moment before they came up for air.

"You know we'll scandalize both our families by staying married to each other," she remarked.

"Who cares? We withstood their attempts to pull us apart."

She nodded. "It's the awful interfamily feud."

Colin smiled, his eyes twinkling. "We're putting it to rest. In fact, I suggest we make love not war right now."

"We're in Sawyer's flat."

Colin looked around them. "Looks good to me. Can you think of something better to do on a wet and overcast day?"

"Colin…"

Belinda laughed as he tugged her down with him to the deep rug before the fireplace, pulling a blanket off the sofa as he did so.

It wasn't long before the weather was forgotten for more interesting pursuits....

Later, Belinda snuggled with Colin on the sofa, watching the rain beat against the windows of Sawyer's London flat.

Colin cleared his throat. "I let revenge take over for three years. It was convenient not to look beyond that overruling motivation."

"Because I walked away." She said the words without rancor, as merely a statement of fact.

Colin lifted the corner of his mouth. "You didn't just walk. You ran."

"What?" she joked. "In three-inch platform heels and a red sequin minidress?"

"The minute I saw you, I wanted to strip you out of them."

She gazed at him through her lashes. "And you did."

"You couldn't have chosen a better seduction ensemble if you had tried," Colin teased. "What were you thinking?"

Belinda heated. "I was thinking that I was in Vegas and I was going to have a good time."

"Ah," he said, nodding with understanding. "You were already starting to do things your way without knowing it."

"And maybe, just maybe, when I saw you, I made sure to stay put until you spotted me in the hotel."

"Ah." Colin nodded with satisfaction. "Finally, a confession. Here's mine—I knew you were staying at the Bellagio."

Belinda's eyes widened. "No doubt your ego was in full bloom."

He placed her hand on his chest. "But my heart shriveled on the vine for the next three years."

She turned her head to look up at him. "Did you ever discover how our annulment was never finalized in Nevada?"

"The biggest confession of all," Colin admitted. "I did not authorize my attorney to file the annulment papers."

Belinda gasped and then laughed in disbelief. "I always suspected as much!"

"I tried to find every which way to get you back. I even pursued the end of the Wentworth-Granville feud in order to get you back. Why do you think I became a collector of impressionist art?"

Belinda's eyes shone. "Me?"

Colin nodded.

Belinda swallowed against the well of emotion. "Oh, Colin, how sweet and romantic."

He brushed her lips with his.

"I'm sorry for running out on you in Vegas." When he made to speak, she pressed a finger to his lips. "In the morning, I was afraid of the floodgates that you opened in me, and I didn't know how to deal with the situation. You were willing to take risks that I wasn't. You were more than I expected, and more than I could handle at the time."

When she lowered her hand, he stole another quick kiss.

"You handled me fine." His eyes glinted. "And I'd say you took a big risk by eloping with me. You just needed me to get used to jumping into the deep end once in a while in your life."

She laughed. "I'm sure you'll give me plenty more chances to do it."

"I was a lord who was missing his heart, and didn't know it."

"The majority of Wentworths would agree that you were heartless," she allowed.

"Only because you'd stolen my heart." He looked deeply into her eyes. "And you absconded to New York with it."

Belinda's lips twitched. "Uncle Hugh would claim you're the thief who stole the Wentworth family patrimony—the London town house, the Berkshire country estate…"

"But what you didn't understand is that you always had the more valuable property in your possession, and I was just trying to get my heart back."

"You took the family jewel, the Berkshire estate."

"The only jewel I stole was you."

"I guess I'll have to change my name to Granville, then."

Colin gave a small smile. "I guess you'll have to, if you want to."

"What? And risk giving people, including your mother, conniptions at being styled Belinda Wentworth, Marchioness of Easterbridge?"

"I wouldn't mind as long as you remained the lady of my heart."

"Oh."

"Would you like to renew our vows?"

Belinda swallowed against the lump in her throat. "I've been a disaster at weddings, in case you haven't noticed."

He gave her a swift kiss. "What matters is that you're a winner at marriage."

"It's nice of you to think so."

He gave her an intimate smile. "I'm betting on it."

Belinda smiled. "Then, yes, I'll marry you again."

"The local parish church would do nicely. The locals will love the show."

"Even if I'm not dressed in red sequins?" she joked.

"Especially if I avoid a white Elvis suit."

She laughed.

"I started out trying to put the Wentworth-Granville feud to rest by vanquishing the Wentworths. Instead, by falling in love, we'll be the means together to end the feud in a far more satisfactory way."

Belinda couldn't agree more. "I can't wait to get started together on your next strategy."

Epilogue

It was the Christmas season in snowy Berkshire, and Belinda was surrounded by those who loved her and whom she loved in return.

What else could a woman ask for?

She surveyed the scene in the sitting room at Halstead Hall. A huge tree hugged one corner of the room, a bright star at the very top and foil ribbon gracing the boughs.

Colin was speaking with Hawk near the tree, but in the next moment, his eyes connected with hers.

A look ripe with emotion and understanding passed between them. Colin's face said that he adored her—and he couldn't wait to get her alone.

Then he winked, and Belinda's smile widened.

She was six months pregnant with twins—a boy and a girl—and this time next year, they would be parents like their friends. It was nice to get a reminder that even in her current state, her husband still, well, *lusted,* for her.

On the floor in front of one of the sofas, Pia played with her son, William, the seven-month-old Earl of Eastchester—the courtesy title used by the eldest son of the Duke of Hawkshire. She laughed along with Tamara when William snagged a ball that had been rolled his way by Tamara's fifteen-month-old son, Elliott Langsford, Viscount Averil.

Off to one side, Tamara's husband, Sawyer, stood with a toddler's juice box in hand, surveying the action.

This time next year, two children would become four, Belinda thought. She'd be playing on the floor along with Pia and Tamara, though it was hard to believe these days since her view of her feet had already disappeared.

She and Colin hoped to make this Christmastime gathering an annual event with the two couples whom they considered the best of friends.

And fortunately, they both continued to mend fences with their families. She and Colin had had a lovely, formal wedding at the local parish church in Berkshire and a reception at Halstead Hall. She'd worn a designer sleeveless gown with white gloves that had drawn a gratifyingly stunned response from Colin. For his part, Colin had exuded a quiet male authority in a morning jacket and red cummerbund.

They had even invited Mrs. Hollings to the wedding. She had turned out to be a sixty-something woman who was a British subject by birth but had lived in New York for years. She also had impeccable sources.

For Belinda, the third time had been the charm, because though both Wentworths and Granvilles had attended, there had been no hiccup in the proceedings. Of course, it had helped that the two families had followed tradition and occupied opposite sides of the church aisle.

Now, however, that Belinda was pregnant with Wentworth-

Granville offspring, even the fact that she'd legally changed her name to Belinda Granville had apparently faded into the background. Even Colin's mother had become reconciled, though, of course, to her, the expected grandchildren were simply Granvilles.

Hawk bent down to help his son, and Colin came over to her and slipped his arm around her back.

"Happy?" Colin asked her.

"Of course," Belinda said. "And it's wonderful to have our friends here with us."

Colin smiled. "Even though both our families are set to arrive the day after Christmas for Boxing Day?"

"They'll behave, or else," she threatened with mock humor.

"If Uncle Hugh bests my mother at chess again, there may be blood on the Persian rug."

Belinda laughed. "Who knew they'd have something in common?"

Uncle Hugh continued to reside at the Mayfair town house and the estates nearby in Berkshire. Eventually the property would pass to Belinda's children, as was always intended.

The Elmer Street property had been sold—Belinda herself had pushed for it—and the proceeds used to upgrade the Berkshire estates and the Mayfair town house.

Belinda knew she was lucky.

She had asked for and gotten a transfer to the London office of Lansing's. She had worked there for several months and given notice only two weeks ago. She hoped, though, to keep her hand in the art world somehow. There were many priceless works of art at Halstead Hall to give her inspiration.

For the moment, however, she had her hands full with the babies' impending arrival, her work with the staff at

Colin's various properties and her charitable and other endeavors as the Marchioness of Easterbridge.

"Life is good," she announced.

"But not like a dappled impressionist painting," Colin teased. "It's more like a work of modern art. It's what you make of it. It's all in the eye of the beholder."

"Kiss me," she said, "and I'll tell you what I make of it."

Colin's eyes twinkled. "I'd love to."

And they sealed their future with a kiss.

* * * * *

PASSION

For a spicier, decidedly hotter read—
this is your destination for romance!

Harlequin® *Desire*

COMING NEXT MONTH
AVAILABLE DECEMBER 6, 2011

#2125 THE TEMPORARY MRS. KING
Kings of California
Maureen Child

#2126 IN BED WITH THE OPPOSITION
Texas Cattleman's Club: The Showdown
Kathie DeNosky

#2127 THE COWBOY'S PRIDE
Billionaires and Babies
Charlene Sands

#2128 LESSONS IN SEDUCTION
Sandra Hyatt

#2129 AN INNOCENT IN PARADISE
Kate Carlisle

#2130 A MAN OF HIS WORD
Sarah M. Anderson

You can find more information on upcoming Harlequin® titles,
free excerpts and more at www.HarlequinInsideRomance.com.

HDCNM1111

REQUEST YOUR FREE BOOKS!
2 FREE NOVELS PLUS 2 FREE GIFTS!

ALWAYS POWERFUL, PASSIONATE AND PROVOCATIVE

YES! Please send me 2 FREE Harlequin Desire® novels and my 2 FREE gifts (gifts are worth about $10). After receiving them, if I don't wish to receive any more books, I can return the shipping statement marked "cancel." If I don't cancel, I will receive 6 brand-new novels every month and be billed just $4.30 per book in the U.S. or $4.99 per book in Canada. That's a saving of at least 14% off the cover price! It's quite a bargain! Shipping and handling is just 50¢ per book in the U.S. and 75¢ per book in Canada.* I understand that accepting the 2 free books and gifts places me under no obligation to buy anything. I can always return a shipment and cancel at any time. Even if I never buy another book, the two free books and gifts are mine to keep forever.

225/326 HDN FEF3

Name _____ (PLEASE PRINT)

Address _____ Apt. #

City _____ State/Prov. _____ Zip/Postal Code

Signature (if under 18, a parent or guardian must sign)

Mail to the Reader Service:
IN U.S.A.: P.O. Box 1867, Buffalo, NY 14240-1867
IN CANADA: P.O. Box 609, Fort Erie, Ontario L2A 5X3

Not valid for current subscribers to Harlequin Desire books.

Want to try two free books from another line?
Call 1-800-873-8635 or visit www.ReaderService.com.

* Terms and prices subject to change without notice. Prices do not include applicable taxes. Sales tax applicable in N.Y. Canadian residents will be charged applicable taxes. Offer not valid in Quebec. This offer is limited to one order per household. All orders subject to credit approval. Credit or debit balances in a customer's account(s) may be offset by any other outstanding balance owed by or to the customer. Please allow 4 to 6 weeks for delivery. Offer available while quantities last.

Your Privacy—The Reader Service is committed to protecting your privacy. Our Privacy Policy is available online at www.ReaderService.com or upon request from the Reader Service.

We make a portion of our mailing list available to reputable third parties that offer products we believe may interest you. If you prefer that we not exchange your name with third parties, or if you wish to clarify or modify your communication preferences, please visit us at www.ReaderService.com/consumerchoice or write to us at Reader Service Preference Service, P.O. Box 9062, Buffalo, NY 14269. Include your complete name and address.

HDES11B

*Lucy Flemming and Ross Mitchell shared a magical,
sexy Christmas weekend together six years ago.
This Christmas, history may repeat itself when they find
themselves stranded in a major snowstorm...
and alone at last.*

Read on for a sneak peek from
IT HAPPENED ONE CHRISTMAS
by Leslie Kelly.

Available December 2011, only from Harlequin® Blaze™.

EYEING THE GRAY, THICK SKY through the expansive wall of
windows, Lucy began to pack up her photography gear.
The Christmas party was winding down, only a dozen or so
people remaining on this floor, which had been transformed
from cubicles and meeting rooms to a holiday funland. She
smiled at those nearest to her, then, seeing the glances at her
silly elf hat, she reached up to tug it off her head.

Before she could do it, however, she heard a voice. A
deep, male voice—smooth and sexy, and so not Santa's.

"I appreciate you filling in on such short notice. I've
heard you do a terrific job."

Lucy didn't turn around, letting her brain process what
she was hearing. Her whole body had stiffened, the hairs on
the back of her neck standing up, her skin tightening into
tiny goose bumps. Because that voice sounded so familiar.
Impossibly familiar.

It can't be.

"It sounds like the kids had a great time."

Unable to stop herself, Lucy began to turn around,
wondering if her ears—and all her other senses—were
deceiving her. After all, six years was a long time, the mind

HBEXP1211

could play tricks. What were the odds that she'd bump into *him,* here? And today of all days. December 23.

Six years exactly. Was that really possible?

One look—and the accompanying frantic thudding of her heart—and she knew her ears and brain were working just fine. Because it was *him.*

"Oh, my God," he whispered, shocked, frozen, staring as thoroughly as she was. "Lucy?"

She nodded slowly, not taking her eyes off him, wondering why the years had made him even more attractive than ever. It didn't seem fair. Not when she'd spent the past six years thinking he must have started losing that thick, golden-brown hair, or added a spare tire to that trim, muscular form.

No.

The man was gorgeous. Truly, without-a-doubt, mouthwateringly handsome, every bit as hot as he'd been the first time she'd laid eyes on him. She'd been twenty-two, he one year older.

They'd shared an amazing holiday season.

And had never seen one another again.

Until now.

Find out what happens in
IT HAPPENED ONE CHRISTMAS
by Leslie Kelly.
Available December 2011, only from Harlequin® Blaze™

Harlequin®

ROMANTIC
SUSPENSE

USA TODAY BESTSELLING AUTHOR

MARIE FERRARELLA

Brings you another exciting installment from

CAVANAUGH
JUSTICE

A Cavanaugh Christmas

When Detective Kaitlyn Two Feathers follows a kidnapping case outside her jurisdiction, she enlists the aid of Detective Thomas Cavelli. Still reeling from the discovery that his father was a Cavanaugh, Thomas takes the case, thinking it will be a nice distraction…until Kaitlyn becomes his ultimate distraction. As the case heats up and time is running out, Thomas must prove to Kaitlyn that he is trustworthy and risk it all for the one thing they both never thought they'd find—love.

Available November 22 wherever books are sold!

www.Harlequin.com

HRS27753